The Reflective Dissent

Tamara Rose Blodgett

All Rights Reserved.
Copyright © 2016 Tamara Rose Blodgett

ISBN: 1539770044
ISBN 13: 9781539770046

No part of this publication may be reproduced, distributed, or transmitted in any form or by any means, or stored in a database or retrieval system, without the prior written permission of the publisher.

This book is a work of fiction. The names, characters, places, and incidents are products of the writer's imagination or have been used fictitiously and are not to be construed as real. Any resemblance to persons, living or dead, actual events, locales, or organizations is entirely coincidental.

www.tamararoseblodgett.com
TRB Facebook Fan Page: www.facebook.com/
AuthorTamaraRoseBlodgett

*Cover art by **Phatpuppyart.com***
*Editing suggestions provided by **Red Adept Editing***

Dedication

Carina

For all your dedication and wonderfulness.

Music that inspired me during the writing of this novel:

Sound of Silence :
https://www.youtube.com/watch?v=u9Dg-g7t2l4

by Disturbed

Directives of the Cause

Seventh: *No death is without consequence*
Eighth: *Defend those who cannot*
Ninth: *Forsake not honor, for it is all that remains*

1

Beth

I am Reflective.

Be that as it may, Beth Jasper is scared. She eschewed the protection of all who would give it. Now she is on Three, in the middle of a time-continuum breach with only herself to blame.

Gunnar, her natural Bloodling father, is cooking within an enchanted patch of forest from the scorching he received from Three's single, strong sun.

The corrupt Reflective, Lance Ryan, has somehow followed her tailwind to this place.

This *time*.

And Chuck, whom she and Merrick dispatched before, has sprung back to life because she dialed them back to a *time* before his demise.

The abuser of Maddie stalks to their location as Ryan corners her.

I am Reflective, Beth repeats.

She does not retreat, though her heart beats its resistance.

"Dickbag!" Jacky screams.

Beth doesn't react, flinch, or move in any way. Chuck is stalking toward them with real purpose, but that is the least of her problems.

"Hello, mongrel," Ryan calls softly, circling where she stands. His tall form is tense—ready. His golden good looks glow softly in the dim shadows, whereas Beth's dark looks must blend with the gloom of the deep shadows provided by the canopy of trees.

"Beth," Gunnar croaks, reaching for her, his liquid gaze following Ryan's progress as he draws nearer.

"We're going," Ryan says in his certain way, and he whips out a small reflective triangle.

Facing away, of course. He can't have Beth reflecting in avoidance.

Beth's breaths are hotly stacked as she searches anywhere for avoidance—she can't let Ryan get his hands on her.

A crash of brush sounds harsh in the near silence. Even the small creatures of the forest know when violence holds its breath for the unnatural birth of tragedy.

Ryan's pale aqua eyes flick to Maddie, and he frowns.

At that exact moment, her stepfather, Chuck, blunders into their circle. "What the fuck, Maddie?" Chuck bellows, his sloppy and vulgar speech hurting the sensitive Reflective hearing.

Ryan flinches.

Beth's blades are naked in her hands, and she backs away from the men, sparing a glance for Gunnar. She's relieved to see he is halfway to healed.

Not near enough to help me. As before, Beth is utterly on her own. She loosens her wrists, ready to slash and hack.

Chuck laughs. "Isn't this fucking perfect?" A loathsome belch bursts out of his thick lips, and he continues, apparently without noticing, absently scratching his thick side. "We've got that loser brother of Chase, and"—he raps his knuckles against his head—"you deliver this little slut into my arms. She ran off with you, huh?" Chuck looks at Jacky.

"Dickbag," Jacky repeats sullenly. But Beth sees his eyes are all for Ryan.

Jacky must understand where the real danger lies.

Beth adjusts her grip on her ceramic daggers.

Ryan seems to notice the minute shift and grins. "I'm going to enjoy taking you apart, Jasper." A vein stands out on his forehead as he inches closer.

Gunnar growls, and Ryan doesn't even bother to look at her father. The scent of Gunnar's singed flesh fills her nostrils, and she knows that he'll need much blood to restore himself.

Chuck surveys his surroundings, his eyes falling to Beth. "And *you*." His beady eyes narrow on her like a target, but she dare not take her eyes from Ryan. "You're back for a lesson in manners. I feel like I've won the lottery." He shrugs, seems to notice his sheers for the first time, and lowers them beside his leg.

Beth tracks for reflection, but the dull blades are smeared in wet grass.

Chuck's beady eyes sweep Ryan then her Bloodling father on the ground.

"What in the Sam Hill is this thing here?" He points the sheers at Gunnar.

Leave my blooded father alone, Swine.

"He is a One in need of elimination," Ryan says in an offhand way, and she feels the whip of heat as he uses the dull and shadowed reflection of the sheers to jump within striking distance of Chuck.

Beth misses the bare spot on the metal but uses Ryan's tailwind. His absolute discounting of her is the thing that wins her time. Others' arrogance has saved her before.

Ryan grips Chuck's neck with one hand. No small thing, as it is thick—like his head.

Beth dips low and pounds her knuckles into Ryan's kidneys like exacting gunfire.

Organ strikes don't hurt instantly.

Ryan whirls, and Beth jumps back out of his extensive reach, her hands throbbing.

"I'll kill you," Ryan manages then drops to his knees, his mouth forming a silent *O*.

Beth spins, kicking him in his exposed jaw. Something cracks, and Beth doesn't wait to figure out how fast he'll heal from the injuries she just gave him.

She leaps backward. "Blood passage!" Beth shouts into the canopy of the trees, praying they know her on Three—as they did on Sector One.

Her arms rise.

The trees don't need a second invitation.

"Maddie—Jacky," Beth hisses, jerking her chin upward.

"Beth Jasper of Papilio," the trees thunder at her. Leaves spiral down from the deep timbre of their collective voices, and her eardrums pulse.

The Threes raise their arms.

"Fuck, that *kills*!" Jacky hollers.

Maddie whimpers as the barbs of the great trees set deep in all their flesh.

"Gunnar," Beth whispers, dropping to her knees, lightheaded. Her fingers bite into the fine, slightly damp moss of the forest floor.

Ryan approaches from behind as Beth is being bled. She can't avoid him, and as she attempts to, the barbs drag at her flesh.

"You bitch!" he shouts, and the breath from his words lifts the fine hairs at her nape, warming her neck.

He latches onto her braid, winding it on his forearm. He'll pull her, and she'll have holes all over her body.

Beth clenches her eyes shut as he begins to drag her backward.

Then the trees bind him as well—at his throat, his arms.

"No!" Ryan bellows at them. To Beth it sounds like an abbreviated gurgle.

"Kind of a harpy, ain't he?" Chuck says to no one in particular.

Chuck is still in the game.

Ryan jerks Beth's head back, and she stifles a scream as the barbs lance her arms, and her scalp sings with painful tension.

Chuck stands above her. "This is too perfect. First, I'm gonna do you, then I'm gonna do her." He jerks his meaty jaw toward Maddie, and she mewls as excess blood runs down her arms in small rivulets. "Her mama didn't tell me where she was hiding, even with all the *encouragement* I offered."

Encouragement with fists, Beth guesses, her scalp on fire.

Chuck looks at Ryan struggling against branches that don't yield. "Where's that gray peckerwood who was cooking?"

Gunnar.

"Father," Beth croaks, beginning to lose consciousness. Too much blood has been spilled to feed the trees, and Ryan's hold is too tight for breath, for thought.

"Right here, spawn of Three." Gunnar stands tall, holding the sheers high. He slices them in a downward arc. The tips pierce the top of Chuck's worthless skull.

Beth's eyes shut, her scalp throbbing as she hears Chuck's mouth open and close. The thrashing of his body disturbs the underbrush as death throes consume him. Finally, his desperate struggles subside.

Beth's lids lift.

Gunnar, seven inches taller than Chuck, twists the closed blades sharply.

Chuck's head moves with the momentum, his neck breaking with a wet snap. Gunnar kicks the abuser in his posterior, and he stumble-walks, his arms outstretched, then falls on his face to the forest floor.

Beth cranes her neck at Gunnar then directs her attention to Ryan. His hold has loosened. He can't maintain it while he's struggling to inhale. Blood is infringing with his breathing. The barbs have sunk too deep.

Where is the mirrored rectangle he had?

A tree branch wraps Ryan's throat tighter, and he chokes, struggling to excise himself. His fingers slide out of her unwoven braid.

Beth wants to rail at him. Tell him he deserves to die. She does none of it.

"Enough!" she says into the silence of the woods. The barbs hurt as they tear out of her arms.

She, Jacky, and Maddie fall forward, their fingertips stabbing the soft earth.

Gunnar moves forward. All that remains of his suffering by sunlight is skin so red it appears sunburned.

No lesions remain.

Beth's exhale is shaky with relief.

"I need blood," he says in a matter-of-fact way.

His eyes move to Ryan.

"No," Beth says automatically. She can't let a Bloodling feed on a Reflective. Even though Ryan's presence means her certain torture and death—even though Ryan corrupted their world—The Cause.

She would be exactly as he is if she allowed that.

Gunnar cups Beth's chin, and Ryan's fingers sink into her hair once more, the only abuse he can inflict.

She grits her teeth against the agony.

Gunnar spins, his hand whipping out in Ryan's direction. His palm connects with the Reflective's chin, snapping his head back against the trunk, stunning him.

Still, his fingers remain latched onto her braid, and Gunnar peels his fingers away and gently lifts her.

"I could have broken his fingers, and I will take blood from the deserving. My kindred blood has given her essence to those of the Tree for safe passage." His shrug clearly says, *It is settled.*

"Don't take Reflective Ryan's blood," Beth manages through her pain.

"Ah, my little hopper"—Beth's Bloodling father smooths from her eyes the hairs that have come loose from the braid—"he will pay in any way I wish."

"No," Beth rasps, shaking her head. Her vision swims with pain, tears, and her body knitting the damage of the barbs.

Gunnar sighs, laying her down on the cool moss at the base of the living trees. Their wide eyes follow him, their lashes blinking like great fronds of fern. "He does not deserve your protection. Look away, Beth.

The Enchanted Forest came to your aid, incapacitated Ryan—for you. Let me take what is mine."

Principle help her, she does. Beth lets a Bloodling feed on a Reflective.

She turns her head away, meeting Jacky's bright green eyes.

"Fuck him, Jasper. It's a damn mercy." Beth doesn't reply to Jacky. Instead, she squeezes her eyes shut.

Damn, damn, damn.

She listens to Gunnar feeding and Ryan's powerful struggle to fight both him and the tree's vice-like grip. Ryan eventually stops thrashing.

Beth's breath stills, and an abiding and profound guilt begins to take hold. She knows her feelings aren't reasonable. That Ryan is evil.

That he meant her death.

But somehow, she's let The Cause down by allowing such a violation against him. *How many directives did I break just now?*

Many.

The insidious sounds of suckling and noisy slurping are the only music of the forest.

When Jacky and Maddie come to where Beth lies, she keeps her eyes closed, and they reach for her at the same time, each putting a hand on her shoulders.

Her emotions wrack through her body, shaking her like the leaves that fall with the murmurings of the magical trees' voices.

2

Slade

As Slade seems to fall without landing, fire and ice extinguish the heat of his body. Chills and fine, needlelike pressure stab along his skin like many fine-toothed insects. Nausea rolls out like a carpet inside his body.

When he lands, it is without finesse but brutal, in a clumsy, arcing thrust upon the sand beside the greatest lake of Sector One.

Slade rises from his hands and knees as nightlopers converge around him and Merrick. His guts beg to evacuate, and his bowels push for release.

Vertigo seizes Slade, and he shakes it off with difficulty. The hopper's method of travel is beyond destabilizing. It's sickening.

He forces his eyes to sweep the nightlopers. Their many half forms of taloned hands and large bodies with heavy muscles are too many to overcome, even with his skill in battle. Even coupled with Merrick's tenacious Reflective skills, they are outnumbered fifteen to two.

Slade casts a lustful gaze over his shoulder at the sparkling grayish-blue water of the great lake of One, knowing Merrick can command a jump from a single reflection off a wave. Of course, thinking that makes him all the more acutely aware of Beth's absence.

"Bad odds, Bloodling." Jeb Merrick states the obvious, his pale gray eyes set on their mutual enemy.

Slade tilts his head, regarding the arrogant Reflective, his bruises already fading. "Brainless comment."

Slade holds his churning stomach, and Merrick grunts, the corner of his mouth twitching.

"Race you to the lake, and there, we can make our way to Beth."

The nightlopers grumble, and their eerie chirps, clicks, and whistles are a symphony of anticipation. They smell blood.

His and the Reflective's.

Slade wonders if Merrick will whisk himself away, leaving Slade to deal with the nightlopers. He sweeps the enemy again. Hyenas are part of the group, gnashing their teeth together, making music with their mouths.

"Yes," Slade answers in a flat hiss, his fangs punching from his gums.

Nightlopers yip and snap, moving in, their teeth grinding, their predatory eyes piercing the male's countenance for weaknesses. The Weres of the group, Lycan in ancestry, growl at the hyenas.

The hyenas are fully formed and the most merciless of the nightloper menagerie. No half forms for that part of the scouting group.

Slade notes the enchanted trees will offer no protection, as he and the Reflective have jumped beyond their purview.

"On my mark." Merrick's quiet tone threads through the air in a whisper.

Slade tenses in readiness, anxious about the potential of being left by the Reflective he doesn't trust. Dead if he stays. Better that he places his trust than not at all.

The hyenas work well as a pack, beginning to circle the lone prey.

I will not be that prey.

Slade inhales deeply, taking in the subtle arid air that heats his lungs, drying his sinuses. He subtly shifts his weight as he catches the scent of those who came shortly before him and Merrick.

Gunnar and Maddie—Jacky.

Beth.

His eyes drift to the forest once more, where bodies of nightlopers fill the soil with their blood. It is enough gore for him to know that blood passage was gifted to them. To Beth.

Merrick uses an ascending whistle to signal Slade.

Slade spins, exploiting the sandy shores like a springing board, and leaps toward the lake.

Excited yelps follow, then Merrick and Slade are hurtling themselves toward shore.

"Love that sucker is finally toast." Jacky grins, admiring Chuck's nearly severed head with a glee typically reserved for an anticipated reward, not the loss of human life.

Beth rounds on him, her fists clenched. No death is perfect. None is preferred. And the seventh directive comes to her with a swift consciousness:

No death is without consequence.

Beth wonders what theirs shall be.

"Whoa!" Jacky stumbles backward, taking in her scowl. "Settle." His wordless gaze scans her features. "Beth—didn't we hate this guy? Correct me if I'm wrong." He whips his long bangs out of his face and spreads his dirty fingers over the borrowed Reflective uniform that is way too big for his now-adolescent frame. "He beat Maddie's mom, hurt her—was *gonna* hurt Mad. His death is *worth*." Jacky's exaggerated exhale disturbs the bangs hanging in his eyes. He folds his arms.

Weakness sweeps Beth, and she sways. *Blood loss.* Her eyes find Ryan, unconscious and bleached of color at the base of a gnarled trunk. Beth looks upward and finds the eyes of many enchanted trees at half-mast. They're satiated by her blood—by Jacky's and Maddie's.

Ryan's.

She covers her face with her hands and feels Gunnar's presence before his hand grips her shoulder, offering her a gentle squeeze.

"My daughter."

I have let a Bloodling feed on a Reflective.

Not too dissimilar from watching a female raped by a male.

Not unlike that at all.

Beth feels the burn of scalding tears behind her lids as she opens her eyes, looking into the flat ebony gaze of her father.

A light breeze winds through the heavy branches of the forest and lifts fine hairs to flutter around her face, chilling her heated skin.

"Do not despair, Beth. Reflective Ryan is evil. He has captured your females and spearheaded the uprising on Papilio." Gunnar's hands cradle her face, and he forces her to hear the truth of his actions. That there is no punishment severe enough for someone willing to hurt others the way Reflective Lance Ryan has.

Her tears hover without falling.

Gunnar says, "I have shown mercy this day. I spared his miserable life."

"Yeah—we should kill him, Beth." Jacky's ready for Ryan's death, as he was ready for Chuck's. Beth is struck by how good a Reflective the boy would make. Emotionally, he is quick to kill. Much quicker than she. Beth's compassion and adherence to The Cause has nearly meant her death dozens of times.

"Do not speak, Jacky," Beth says, and her father's hands fall from her cheeks.

Maddie walks to them, her eyes skating briefly to Chuck's corpse and the still-prone figure of Ryan. "Is he…?" Maddie seems reluctant to fully form the question, cupping her elbows as she gives the Reflective furtive glances.

As one, their eyes move to Ryan. His huge body is splayed awkwardly over the tangle of tree roots, and he appears to sleep, his skin like polished alabaster, his chest still of breaths.

Beth concentrates, sensing that his life remains. Ryan's essence ebbs like a flickering flame, but she knows he will survive the bloodletting of her father—the trees' deep drink of his blood.

What would Jeb do?

Merrick has claimed her as his soul mate. He is the leader in their Reflective coupling. Their partnership bound them first, and now his timepiece has bound them further.

Jacky circles her, seeking her gaze.

She gives it and feels her eyes widen in shock that he's back to thirteen cycles. All the sullen and full-fledged glory of a Three teen restored.

Principle. Beth rubs her eyes with the heels of her hands.

"What?" the teen asks, his hand to his chest.

Gunnar remains silent but has definitely noticed the change since One in the boy.

However, her father's ebony eyes hold a mirth Beth doesn't share.

Maddie says, "You look like a teenager again."

"Aww, *shee*-it." Jacky blinks once, raising his hands. He quickly surveys the parts of his body he can see and curses. He kicks a bit of moss under his sneaker, and it upturns like a springy, bright green wound underneath his toe.

The trees come to life, as though waking from a fitful slumber. Their bulbous eyes narrow at him, their deep green "eyelashes" fluttering against heavily furrowed knobs of wood that resemble cheekbones.

"Jacky—" Maddie says in warning, her eyes skating to the trees' clear discontent.

"Disrupt not our home" comes the braying voice of the tree closest to them, its eyelashes sweeping down, blinking over glaring irises that glow with luminescent emerald fire, even the "whites" hold a pale green hue.

Beth protectively covers her ears from the grating timbre.

Gunnar's eyes tighten, and she knows that her sensitive Reflective hearing is made even more acute by her Bloodling heritage.

"He apologizes," Beth says, slowly lowering her hands.

"What?" Jacky asks. "I disrupt a little moss and suddenly"—he whips around his arms, still scarred by the thorns—"I'm in the doghouse." He conducts a slow revolution.

It appears as if the tree could frown, it would. As Beth watches, the nose of the nearest tree hikes, as though sniffing its disdain at the tactless youngling.

Beth glowers at Jacky. "He means no disrespect."

"Pfft." Jacky sounds off, erasing her attempt at defusing the tension.

Maddie grabs his arm. "Quit it."

Jacky folds his arms and huffs.

"This posturing is unhelpful. Let us go." Gunnar throws his hand out, indicating the obvious—a dead body and an unconscious Reflective don't bode well for them.

Gunnar is right.

Beth doesn't wish to engage Ryan again. Creating distance and reuniting with Jeb is better.

"We'll need to travel through the forest belts. You can't deal with this sun," Beth says.

Gunnar smirks. "Apparently not. A most painful experience." He shudders, absently rubbing his broad chest. Great patches of his skin slough off onto the undergrowth of the forest. As Gunnar's skin heals, the dead flesh flakes off.

"That's unattractive as hell. You look like a damn snake," Jacky says, flicking a piece of dead skin off the shoulder of his hoodie.

Maddie moves to Gunnar's side, and Beth can feel his need for her. Though with her own timepiece ticking, Beth wishes she had the intuition she has for others for herself. She doesn't know what might happen between her and Merrick. Slade.

She releases an exhale of pure frustration from between her lips. "We have been granted blood passage."

Gunnar nods. "For now," he says with grave significance.

Beth gives her father a sharp look. "What do you mean?"

Gunnar clasps his hands behind his back. "The trees' patience is not limitless. And there will be areas where the enchantment fades and our sentinels are few and far between. Where they do not exist."

Then not always safe, Beth thinks. Safe for now. However, in the near future…

"Let's go, Beth."

Beth glances at Ryan again. Still for now.

"Maddie wants to check on her mom, Jasper."

She nods. It is only right that Maddie has that closure. Especially since they were unfairly torn from their home world. Beth's eyes run over Maddie, looking wholly Reflective. Looking *other*. She does not fit within Three norms.

Principle, damn.

"Maddie, though Jacky was affected by the time shift, your changes appear to be permanent."

Maddie swallows. "I still look—different."

Gunnar clears his throat, his chin lifting imperceptibly. "You look like a Reflective female in her prime."

His eyes glitter, and Beth stifles an urge to roll her eyes. Are all Bloodling males so caught up in mating and war? Is that all there is?

Then Beth remembers that *her* role is nothing more than a glorified interdimensional police enforcer, with the proverbial dangling carrot of a soul mate as motivator.

It's a healthy motivation.

The Cause trembles at the back of her mind, integrity through training and want all that matters now, as Commander Rachett is nowhere to be found.

Beth bites her lip. "We've moved back in time, Jacky. I don't know how far back."

Jacky's eyes suddenly brighten. "My parents?"

Beth holds up a palm, glancing in Ryan's direction. "I simply don't know."

"Chuck knew you," Maddie states.

Gunnar's polished obsidian gaze lands on her as Maddie's own skitters nervously away.

Beth ignores their exchange. "Which means it was after he tortured me and…after he murdered your parents," Beth states in a hushed voice.

Jacky's shoulders slump, and Beth instantly regrets her matter-of-fact recounting. "I apologize."

His direct, bright green gaze meets hers. "It's okay. I fucking couldn't be that lucky. Chase gone—my parents. Sucks balls." He jams his hands in his denims front pockets, dropping his gaze.

Beth's sigh is long.

Her scrutiny of Ryan is short. *Has his coloring brightened from the color of bleached bones to something less… dead looking?*

"I am not afraid of the Reflective." Gunnar seems to understand her hesitancy. "I can end him."

So might Beth. She reaches out and captures his arm.

He turns slightly and covers her flesh with his own. "Let me give you peace. I have fed from him. Though he is male, his blood was tasty."

Beth watches his black pupils grow wide, within irises just as black. She swallows.

Tasty.

"No. If I am the only one who stands by The Cause, then let it be me."

His upper lip lifts with clear distaste. "The Cause. That is the thing which ultimately ruined your mother."

Beth flinches.

Gunnar frowns, gently taking her hands in his own. "I will not kill this vile male. But if he chooses to come after us, I will end him." Their eyes meet. "Slowly."

"You will not have to," Beth whispers, desperately trying not to think about her partner—and when and where Merrick might be.

"I think it's a bigtime mistake for us to leave this chode alive," Jacky says, kicking his head in Ryan's direction.

Beth agrees, though killing a Reflective is grievous. And cowardly, given his state of consciousness. No matter how awful a male he is, and how unworthy Ryan is to share the same uniform as she, Beth must have integrity.

Gunnar nods, seeming to sense her decision. His hand comes out, and Maddie fills it with her own.

Jacky and Beth follow them. She gives one last look at Ryan, knowing she should kill him, but The Cause holds her fast.

She cannot kill an undefended being in cold blood. Even though Ryan deserves it more desperately than any other.

As they traverse the green belt of enchanted woods in Three, Beth gradually takes the lead. They move toward Maddie's former domicile on the east hill of the Kent Quadrant. Twigs, leaves, and gentle moss give underneath their footprints as thirst and hunger seep into every pore of their tired bodies.

How will Maddie explain her changed appearance to her mother or anyone else they might encounter? An appearance which is too far outside what is considered normal to this world? From Beth's studies of Three, there are no humans with true bluish-purple eyes. And her new shade of inky black locks, though not considered attractive on Papilio, showcases even more the changed appearance between the contrast of her striking eyes and dark hair.

Further, if Beth were a guessing woman, she cannot imagine an instance where her Bloodling father would let his kindred blood go. Having one kindred in a lifetime, finding that elusive mate, is rare.

A second one presenting herself?

Beth would speculate that the happenstance of that would be unprecedented.

Gunnar's eyes travel Maddie possessively. No, Gunnar would not allow her to remain where he is not. Beth feels it in her marrow. If Maddie would raise Threes' eyebrows, Gunnar would cause a riot.

Unless Maddie were to choose where she wanted to be. And therein lies the problem. Maddie is now Reflective but originally from Three.

Gunnar is pure Bloodling.

Madeline DeVere cannot be allowed back into Sector One. It is unsafe for females of any kind, unless they live in the vast safeholding of LaRue, which Slade presided over as the Bloodling Prince.

Nor would she be able to remain in her home world easily.

So where can Maddie belong?

Merrick

Slade rolls over to his hands and knees, and Jeb rises, ignoring the Bloodling heaving his guts onto the lichen-filled forest floor.

Instead, Jeb scans the dense woods, hitting on the magic without too much difficulty.

And Beth's scent.

Extracting his small and deadly ceramic blade from a hidden sheath within his dark navy uniform pants, he notes Slade's eyes widen on the weapon. He staggers to his feet, ready to defend himself against Jeb.

Then promptly vomits again.

Black, partially digested blood spews out, covering the pine needles and other forest debris in what appears like steaming ebony oil.

Jeb would laugh if anything was remotely funny. However, it is not. His soul mate and partner is somewhere on Three—he smells her—and so is Ryan.

His eyes narrow on Slade and his mess. He dragged along the Bloodling only for backup's sake.

Jeb *will locate* Beth, then jump them all back to One. Procure Commander Rachett, then make certain Reflectives Calvin, and Kennet—upon his return to Papilio—are coordinating things correctly on his home world.

He pinches the bridge of his nose. Everything is so—as Jacky would say—fucked up.

Slade slaps his palm on the trunk of a nearby tree and hauls himself upright.

Jeb tenses. If the tree is enchanted, it will be insulted. Nothing stirs, and Jeb feels his muscles gradually unwind. His tumultuous thought processes begin again. Kennet is on One.

Beth is here.

Jeb feels the scowl overtake his face. She left in stealth. Against his express orders.

Why?

"This hopping you Reflectives do is miserable," Slade grates, spitting phlegm onto the spreading pool at his feet.

Jeb folds his arms, planting his feet wide, hating his own smell. "Only to those who do not hold a bit of jumping blood." He hikes an eyebrow at the male.

Slade frowns, wiping his mouth with the back of a hand and taking a moment to retighten the hair club at his nape. "Be that as it may, I loathe becoming sick, *and* the need for blood is more acute, hopper."

Jeb grunts. "Gather your wits, Bloodling, because we need to find Beth."

Slade inspects their environment while Jeb searches the pockets of his retrieved uniform for a locator. "As though I was unaware, Merrick."

Damn.

Frustrated, he looks up, striding to the forest's edge, and searches the outlying area.

Grave markers stand like forgotten tablets of stone on gently sloping hills of grass that are beginning to lose the velvet green of this sector's summer. Afternoon sunlight drains to the shadows of the upcoming night.

Jeb's eyes move back then stutter over an angelic carved marble statue that marks an imposing mausoleum.

The horn shines from the hands of the angel, the late day's sunrays casting useable reflections everywhere.

He blinks. *I know exactly where we are.*

Jeb senses something and whirls.

Slade stands right behind him. He straightens, mute. It's quite a feat for the gray-skinned Bloodling to look ashen, but he manages it.

Jeb frowns, a vague idea rising when Slade interrupts his thoughts.

"What have you discovered, hopper?"

Jeb feels his face tighten. "Address me as Merrick."

Flat black eyes meet his own, and the Bloodling ever so slightly inclines his head. "Then you must call me Slade."

Jeb slowly nods, and a tense truce of sorts ensues. He turns back to the graveyard view, the exact spot where he and Beth had jumped before this whole new mess began.

Sunlight appears to spill like blood over the green grass. "We have jumped to Three, the quadrant of America and the lesser quadrant of Kent, Washington."

"Why?" Slade asks, his voice raspy from vomiting.

He turns partially. "I caught Beth's tailwind. She travels with Gunnar, Jacky, and Maddie. I can only presume she is leaving the Threes in their world of origin."

Slade slides his jaw back and forth, stating the obvious. "That's foolish. Maddie appears as a Reflective female."

Jeb turns fully, and they face off. "Not wholly."

"Do not"—Slade palms his chin—"split hairs, as the Threes call it. She does not look like the humanoids who reside here."

"And you've visited Three so often?" Jeb folds his arms.

Slade gives a slight shake of his head. "No," he says shortly, "but there are those who've hopped before, taking evidence. Proof of the differences among sectors."

Jeb did not know that others had jumped with enough precision to detail history, or survey anything, doing nothing other than maim and plunder. The very thing The Cause was erected to prevent. Disquiet coats his guts like sour milk. But Jeb does not voice his misgivings. Not with a Bloodling.

"Let's follow their trail. We will meet up with them, ascertain Beth's well-being, and jump her to Papilio."

Slade shakes his head. His black hair is loose around his shoulders, and he's in dire need of a cleanser, as is Jeb. His wounds from the torture and beating he suffered heal excruciatingly slowly. Many of the surface injuries are faded, but the deep bruising and internal bleeding will take more time. Food and rest is needed. But his soul mate is away from him and unprotected.

Slade tears a tie from the pocket of his tunic, once again slicking the inky strands of hair back and turning them tightly at his nape, where he secures everything into a neat hair club.

Slade's cool dark gaze finds Jeb, his nostrils flaring hard. "First, we discover what smells like chilling blood and rotting meat."

Jeb's eyebrows rise. All Reflectives have an acute sense of smell.

Slade claps him on the back, and Jeb fights not to lurch forward at the abrupt contact.

"Can't smell it, Merrick?" Slade is grinning now.

Jeb would very much like to wipe that expression from the Bloodling's face. His eyes narrow on the large male.

Slade tilts his head, indicating Jeb should follow. After a moment's hesitation, he hikes after him. Trudging about a quarter kilometer deeper into the woods, they see something.

There, at the base of a large and ancient tree trunk, a body lies. Head canted to the extreme left, it appears as though nearly torn from its thick neck.

As Jeb draws nearer, he recognizes the corpse, and his lips draw away from his teeth in disgust. "What in Principle's name?" he mutters, sinking to his haunches. His eyes roam the wounds. Jeb frowns, recognizing the killing style.

"Merrick?" Slade asks, his voice urgent.

Jeb cranes his head, looking up at the giant Bloodling. "This is Maddie's sire," he explains, slipping smoothly into the Sector One tongue.

Slade tips his head back. "Ah." His lips curl. "He does not look like he's much of anything now."

Jeb nods, standing. "He was not her." Jeb struggles. Some of the words to describe difficult references do not come readily to him, and a pang of longing for Beth spears through him. "Biological father," Jeb finishes finally.

That seems only to confuse Slade more. "Who ended him?"

Judging by the wound, it would be Gunnar, but Jeb frowns, gazing at the neck. That wound is ceramic kissed—he recognizes it.

Not that Beth couldn't accomplish this fool's death—or want to. But the wound's depth of the near decapitation speaks to leverage gained by height and superior strength—not talent, skill, and expertise, all of which Beth possesses.

The raw execution indicates speed and necessity were factors, which causes Jeb to search the deep pockets of the woods more thoroughly for the other scent he had identified.

Ryan.

Jeb's nostrils flare, and the scent of the other Reflective tingles his nostrils.

He unsheathes his second ceramic dagger, giving a sideways glance to Slade.

Slade goes from neutral to aggressive in a moment, dipping his chin. "I smell the hopper."

They exchange a full glance.

When he finds a partial answer for why the Reflective's scent still lingers but he's not here, Jeb rubs a hand over his skull. Fine hairs bristle underneath the contact.

"This is bad."

Jeb glares at Slade as their attention clings to a section of matted-down moss that nestles between the roots of the great tree. The moss is in the shape of a large male.

Ryan was here.

Slade moves to the area, and lowering himself to his knees, he closes his eyes, inhaling deeply. "He was bled."

Jeb presses his fingertips against the deeply furrowed tree.

Their eyes meet.

"Gunnar?" Jeb asks incredulously, resheathing his daggers.

Slade gives a laugh like a bark. "That is my deduction."

Jeb's disquiet deepens. "Beth would not allow that."

Slade smirks. "I think our Beth is doing what she must to survive. And why would she protect that deplorable hopper?" Slade's eyes simmer with remembered hate. "A rapist and murderer of his own kind? Do you not recall the illegal fighting? How he intended to beat Beth to death? A female?"

Our Beth.

Jeb would never forget Ryan seeking to kill Beth. Just as he would not readily forget Slade's treachery to see him out of the picture.

Jeb's chin kicks up. "He *will* be held accountable."

Slade grins suddenly. "By whom? The defunct Cause?" Slade makes a sound of harsh disbelief then coughs. "No. Your Commander Rachett has been given to the nightlopers of my world. They would have torn his limbs off by now and beaten him with the bloody stump."

Jeb hates his truths but can't deny the potential logic within.

Slade stands, hitching up pants made of skinned animals, straightening his tunic, and puts his powerful hands on his hips. "I say we go after this Reflective"—he spits the word out like a foul taste in his mouth—"and kill him solely for the sake of rendering the collective sectors free of his stain. Then—we secure Beth."

The wheels of Jeb's mind turn. "How do you know Ryan was bled?"

Slade's eyebrows jerk in surprise. "Too clean, Merrick."

Merrick's eyes scan the ground. Not one drop of red can be seen in the sea of green forest floor.

"What would cause Gunnar to feed on a male?" Jeb knows that feeding by a male Bloodling is almost exclusively from a female.

Slade shakes his head. "Need. Extreme need. Taking from a male outside of battle is…"—his lips lift off sharp, brilliant white teeth and short fangs—"distasteful."

Jeb does not suck blood as the Bloodlings do, of course, but he has no desire for male flesh in general. He understands the male Bloodlings' disinterest from taking from their own gender.

Suddenly Slade lifts his face, taking in the sun as it sets, partially revealed through the thick canopy of trees. "How many suns?"

Jeb frowns then understands. "Sector Three has one powerful star."

Shrewd eyes address him. "*Ah*—but Gunnar would not necessarily know that or remember. He forgot himself and must have"—Slade looks outside the border of trees to the vast rolling steep hills beyond—"gone into the sun."

Jeb's sense of urgency reasserts itself. "It's not relevant. Let's go. Their trail cools."

Slade captures Jeb's arm, and his eyes stare pointedly at the contact. "Gunnar will not take to you ordering Beth around or doing the same to Madeline. He's claimed her as kindred blood."

Jeb shakes off his large hand and begins walking where the beat of his soul mate pulses, some distance from their position.

Ryan's as well.

"I cannot help the needs of the bonded Reflective male. My very basest instincts will not be satisfied until I see her safe."

He spins to Jeb, and Slade's dark eyes are slits of black within the deeply shadowed woods, as though they've disappeared. "Nor I, Merrick."

Merrick steps into his advance, gritting his teeth. "You have no claim on Beth."

"And her timepiece still ticks away. Ticktock." Slade's voice clucks with soft precision.

Jeb's arms straighten, his hands curling into fists. "She is unprotected while you argue with me about schematics and circumstance."

"Tiny Frog is a warrior, and her *warrior* father is with her. Ryan can *try*. And that is all that will happen. Between the two of them, she is well protected."

Jeb lets a disgusted breath slide out of him. "That is what separates us, Bloodling. You desire Beth for superficial reasons. I desire her forever."

Jeb turns away from the Bloodling again.

He cannot count on the male as anything other than an in-the-moment protection of Beth.

If she needs it.

Beth Jasper is Reflective, and that is no small thing. Jeb wishes desperately that the one who followed her was not.

4

Beth

Tears stream down Maddie's face, dripping unheeded from her chin. Her jewel-colored iolite gaze travels the disheveled mess surrounding them.

The dwelling Madeline DeVere shared with her mother appears to have been completely ruined, as though a human tornado spun through.

The front door hangs off its hinges like a decaying tooth, twitching in its jamb as they attempt to pry it forward. The bottom shrieks as it's dragged across the floor.

"Fucking *Chuck*," Jacky spits, kicking a torn pillow. It flies across the main part of the dwelling, ironically falling on an upturned couch.

Maddie moves forward, obviously intending to search the domicile.

"Don't, Mad." Jacky captures her arm.

She whirls toward him, her finger raised. "Don't tell me what I can't see. I won't be protected anymore. Chuck is gone—*this* is my home." More angry tears rush like train tracks down her face, and Beth sighs.

"Shit," Jacky mutters, grabbing his nape and casting his eyes down. When he raises that emerald stare, his attention moves to Gunnar.

A look passes between them that's impossible not to interpret—*Maddie's mother.*

Gunnar's eyes widen.

Beth moves fast, faster than any of them, catching Maddie against her.

"No!" Maddie wails.

Beth tips her forehead against the taller girl's back, holding her fast about the waist. Though Maddie is taller, Beth's four times stronger than a Three female.

"I know he's hurt her!" Maddie yells, kicking her legs up and squirming to get loose. Her wet anguish soaks through Beth's borrowed clothes.

"Let me look for your kin," Gunnar says at Beth's elbow, and he reaches out, cupping her wet face.

Maddie stills. Blinks. Finally, after a brutally tense minute, she nods and relaxes against Beth's hold.

Gunnar holds her eyes a heartbeat longer, then with a terse nod, he leaves them.

They wait for Gunnar's investigation with their collective breaths held.

Finally Gunnar returns, his lips set in a grim line.

When Maddie sees Gunnar's expression, she crumples against Beth.

Gunnar comes to her, pulling her into his huge arms. "There, there, blood of my blood," he soothes, and she chokes back her cries, clearly willing herself to be brave.

Maddie finally stops crying and pulls away, looking up into the Bloodling's face. "Is she…" Maddie bites her bottom lip as fresh tears well after the old.

Gunnar is silent.

"I have to see."

Gunnar doesn't say no, but every bit of his body tenses. "It is not—" He curses from low and deep in his throat, and Beth watches as his fangs descend. "This is not what I would want someone I care for so deeply to witness. And that a male did this to a female…" His fists clench, a low hiss escaping his lips.

Gunnar gives Beth a glance that freezes her insides.

Maddie's hands cover her face, and he grips her, pulling her in against his chest. "You can never forget evils that you consume with your eyes, Madeline. However, in this moment, you can choose what you must partake of. And this bit of violence, I would spare you if I could."

He drops his arms, and she steps away.

Their eyes lock, and for a moment, Beth thinks Maddie might turn and walk out the front door.

She doesn't.

Instead, Maddie walks around where Gunnar stands, as though he's guarding her from herself, and steps over the debris of her home.

Beth hears crunching glass and a clunking sound of wood being stumbled over.

Gunnar's eyes shut as she passes, his shoulders slumping in defeat.

Beth knows when Maddie finds her mother.

The very air trembles with her grief.

They are silent as they make their way to Jacky's domicile, hardly a kilometer from where Madeline lives.

Gunnar doesn't carry Maddie, but it is an emotional cost not to. Instead, he holds her hand, dragging her unresponsive body behind him. Her vacant eyes look with dispassionate interest around them. There isn't much of a view.

Beth has kept to the wide ribbons of greenbelts, which hold thickly wooded forests between rows of what Beth knows they call "houses" here on Three. To Beth's Papilion eye, they appear cheap and without heart.

She longs for her domicile on Papilio, with its stone construction and wooden beams. Her butterflies. Windows with a view of the grape vineyards growing out of the rolling hills in the distance.

Gunnar obviously would look alien, and that is another viable reason to stick to the shadows. Beth shivers. The kind of notice they'd receive because of who she travels with would be unacceptable.

Certainly without a locator, she'll have to manually jump them back to One or Papilio. And that is always a risky proposition. The single most critical thing drilled into the candidates, from the time they began reflecting at the tender age of five cycles, was to always jump with a locator.

Always reflect with a partner.

And here is Beth, partnerless and without a locator. To use a typical Three saying—shooting blind.

I will not allow myself to think of Jeb. Of Slade.

Yet they creep inside the fissures of her troubled psyche. Especially what Slade made her feel. Her body aches for his touch, and Beth understands deep down that lust and passion are not enough. He's awakened something inside her, true. And though he's proven not to hurt her, a nagging bit of herself doesn't wholly trust his motives. She feels there are things Slade keeps from her, and certainly there are things he keeps from Jeb. And Merrick, though having declared her, is still, foremost, her partner. Beth longs for friendships and knows that yearning weakens her. Blinds her to the others' motivations that might not be pure.

"Holy shit," Jacky whispers.

Beth halts, scanning his neighborhood and remembering the last time she was in that house. The day they jumped here had been some sort of strange holiday where Three younglings traipsed around in costume and begged for sugared treats.

Beth did not like the tradition.

The group slows, staring up the steep ravine and into the backyard of Jacky's domicile.

Spirals of twisted gray smoke crawl upward—his house is standing in ruins, and a sense of foreboding sweeps Beth. Has Ryan guessed they would come here? Perhaps *he* was the one murdering Madeline's mother—burning down the house where Jacky's parents had lived.

She jumps to these conclusions like skipping stones across a lake. Reflectives are taught to look at coincidences as connections, not random circumstances.

Beth turns to Gunnar, and his broad back swells with his measured breaths. "Gunnar."

He turns, revealing only his profile. "My daughter."

Beth smiles without meaning to. With all the tragedy, the separation from Merrick and her uncertain future, this one man has decided to own their tie. The connection feels more right than it should. Beth breathes through her growing feelings for Gunnar, reminding herself that she was essentially an orphan. Then reprimanding herself that Gunnar had never known of her existence.

Beth forces herself to the present. "I believe Ryan might be behind"—she struggles, unwilling to remind Madeline about the fresh tragedy—"some of the recent happenings."

Jacky walks over, careful not to trip on the sloping ground, toward a drainage ditch that holds excess water runoff.

He jabs a finger behind him, and their eyes travel over the charred wood that was once walls. "Why would Ryan burn our house? My parents are gone." He shrugs, trying for a bravado Beth sees clearly he doesn't embrace.

Jacky crosses his arms. "This Ryan dick? He's Reflective. And you guys—Kennet, Colin, and for sure uptight Merrick—you've made damn sure I know how expert and deliberate ya all are, right?"

Beth doesn't like his tone, but she can't argue the facts. Reflectives are warriors. It's a simple precept.

With a swift nod from her, he goes on.

"And there's no way after Gunnar munched on him, he was feelin' all spry and shit. He wouldn't be able to get here before us, take the time to burn everything down then lie in wait? Nah," he squints up through the tree trunks to the backyard where his house once stood, and only naked, charred two-by-four studs remain. "This is something else. And Ryan's still out there, digging for some payback." He shakes his head, running his fingers through his long dirty-blond hair.

After a few seconds, Gunnar reluctantly admits, "I agree with the youngling."

Beth hides a smile. There is nothing funny about what happened to Jacky's domicile. But Beth is struck by how ridiculous the situation has become. She also realizes her exhaustion plays a role.

Her Bloodling father is here on Three, where she naively thought she'd return Maddie and Jacky. She has no partner, no locator, and a Reflective who wants her dead or, worse, may have roused himself by now. It would take a lot for Ryan to build up his blood after what Gunnar did.

What I allowed. A smart Reflective would jump back to Papilio and recoup, then think about options.

However intelligent Ryan may be, he's lost to his vendetta against her. He won't jump back and use logic. Ryan will press toward her. And now that he knows Jeb has declared her, he'll redouble his efforts.

Beth's mind isn't sharp, her time on One having obviously dulled it. And the horrors of what's transgressed in her own world helps that along.

Think, Beth.

Why would Madeline's mother be dead and Jacky's domicile destroyed? Figuring out the *why* of what's transpired shouldn't matter. But her warrior's brain nags at her. Some niggling bit of unease is trying to warn her there is more to what's happened here than just a superficial event.

"It is almost as though someone is destroying evidence."

Beth turns to Jacky, a sheet of gooseflesh coating her skin as she remembers his well-above-average IQ. "What did you say?" Though she heard him.

Jacky yanks his head back toward the still-smoldering ruins of his house. "What if you guys leave a 'footprint' of having jumped from place to place?"

Of course they do. But only a Reflective could note such proof of their jumping.

Jacky studies her face. "So ya do? You leave some kind of trail of bread crumbs."

Beth feels her face screw up. Gunnar's expression matches her own.

Jacky's exhale is impatient. "I thought you knew earth slang and shit."

Beth frowns at the boy. "I do. But not all. I am expert in all the explored sectors' languages. But some slang"—she lifts a shoulder—"escapes even my ability to interpret."

"Okay, ya get lost in the woods," he begins to explain.

Beth nods, moving her hand in a circle of impatient encouragement.

He holds up a palm. "And you want someone to pick up your trail, so you chuck little pieces of bread for that person to find." His light eyebrows spring up.

Gunnar snorts. "Or a hungry animal to eat."

"Shut up," Jacky says, and Gunnar growls.

"Sorry, big dude, but this is one of those things where it's more an idea than a literal thing, ya feel me?"

Gunnar blinks, and Beth feels momentary sympathy. He is getting to know the Jacky they all did at first blush, and he can be tiresome.

"Jacky," Maddie speaks for the first time, "you're not being very nice."

Jacky and Beth watch her take Gunnar's hand. He looks down at her, smiling, and that bit of fang that all Bloodlings possess peeks out from behind his lips.

Maddie's pulse speeds at the hollow of her throat, and her pupils dilate. The Three female behaves as though she's drugged in the presence of Gunnar. Beth's eyes shift to him.

He is no less affected.

Beth wonders if this is how Merrick is affected by her. If that is so, he has been very careful not to let on the full extent of his feelings.

"It's not about *nice*. Listen, since all this paranormal bullshit came down, there's been a lot of behind-the-scenes speculating about big brother and all that."

Now Beth is well and truly stumped. "Big Brother?"

"Yeah, ya know—government spooks."

Ah yes, Beth remembers the phrase is a crude description of legitimate government having a covert subsection. Usually for deeds they don't want to be accountable for.

He shrugs. "I think this might fall under that."

They look to the destroyed domicile.

"Chuck killed my mom, Jacky."

Jacky walks over to her, and Gunnar tenses, then Beth. She does not want to protect the Three against her newfound relative.

"Chill, big guy." He turns to Maddie. "Listen, Mad. You're a Dimensional, and then you went to Papilio and you ended up being what they classify as Reflective. But here on our earth"—Jacky glances at a silent Beth—"all us teenagers who've been dosed with the DNA cocktail to make paranormal markers manifest within our hidden genes or whatever—we're being observed. Maybe groomed, you get it?"

Beth frowns. They took care of the criminal scientists—the Zondorae brothers. Their plan of total sterilization won't be realized. It was one of her and Jeb's most critical first assignments when they were paired, preempting a dark, barren future for Three.

"I do get it," Beth replies slowly. "But that should no longer be a factor."

The fine machinations of Jacky's mind revolve. Beth sees them plainly on his open expression. "Okay, so you and Merrick came here and changed some shit."

Beth doesn't answer.

Jacky smirks. "Bingo. But anyway, maybe you didn't change enough, and there's someone that noticed that a Dimensional suddenly vanished, and her dead boyfriend's little brother's *parents* were murdered and *why*."

Principle help them.

"So somebody that matters found out enough of the *why*. And they have an idea about you guys." He points at Beth then taps his temple. "And maybe they're working really hard to find you—and Papilio."

Beth's heart rate begins to speed, and the dense forest seems to close in around her—claustrophobic.

"That would be disastrous," Gunnar comments unnecessarily.

Yes it would.

"Did ya ever run into Threes? I mean, besides me and Maddie? When you guys jumped here?"

Beth remembers the reanimated corpse, the female law woman they encountered—the gang that nearly killed her—where she and Jeb jumped through a piece of a shattered automotive side mirror to escape.

"Yes," she says slowly, explaining some of what she can and keeping much of it to herself. She is still a Reflective of The Cause. Speaking about their soldiering is not done.

"So you think a female cop is just going to say *ho-hum,* as you and Merrick hit a broken car mirror on the side of a car and, poof, you vanish? Y'know." He pauses, scratching his head. "She's not gonna just chalk it up as one of those things." He snorts.

Beth locks her hands behind her back. "Merrick and I assumed they would identify us as Dimensionals. After all, by your own admission, paranormal talents are rampant in Three." She shrugs. They went in knowing those facts. She and Jeb were counting on it for the sake of blending in with the locals.

He nods. "Yeah, they are. But Dimensionals don't go through glass, Beth." His eyes are bright in the gloom as they study her. "They jump, like Reflectives…in a way. But they're not jumping through locators mounted on buildings and lakes and that." He rolls his eyes.

"I think we should get the hell out of here and back to Papilio," Jacky says, and Maddie's inhale is shaky.

"I thought you couldn't wait to get to Three?" Beth asks in a low voice, though she keeps sarcasm at bay. His parents were murdered, and the only home he knows is gone. Now is not the time to teach lessons. Life has been an apt teacher.

He shakes his head. "I'll miss my homeboys, and maybe someday I can come back, but if I've got government wackos looking for me and bringing out the big dogs?" He shakes his head. "I'd be safer on Papilio—older."

It's not lawful to remove Threes from their home world. But where does the law end and justice begin? Can she leave the two of them without protection, resources, or family? If Jacky is only thirteen cycles here, in this time, who will tend him until he's grown?

Beth dips her head, taking a few, deep breaths.

"I don't want to go back to Papilio," Maddie says into the deepening gloom.

Beth gives a sharp look to her, then Gunnar.

"No," Beth says, and Gunnar spreads his arms. "I can't deny our tie, Beth Jasper. Mine to you"—he shifts to Maddie—"hers to me."

Maddie steps away from Gunnar.

His shocked expression would be funny if Beth didn't know better. A male Bloodling in the throes of a kindred blood tie is not something to be taken lightly.

Maddie puts her shoulders back. "I'm not going to Sector One, either."

Jacky laughs.

And Gunnar hisses. But not at Jacky—at something else entirely.

There's no time to worry about a lover's spat.

Voices carry down to them from above, and Beth pivots where she stands, automatically securing better footing.

Bright LED spears of light slice the dusk like blistering knives.

Instinctively, Beth searches for reflection—any reflection—to spot jump them away from the intrusion.

Nothing. *Principle.*

Then the unexpected happens.

Ryan, in the clothes of this sector, reveals himself at the top of the hill. "That's them," he says, using perfect Three language.

His grin is malicious.

Beth's gut tightens as Three men start climbing down the incline toward them with weapons of this world.

And she can't reflect anywhere.

5

Merrick

They move like well-suited partners instead of tolerant enemies through the murk of trees that separates Three dwellings from one another.

With perhaps only ten meters of dense tree cover, Slade and Jeb stay tight to each other, their shoulders almost brushing as they make their way toward the combined scent of the others.

Jeb reluctantly concedes that Slade and he are not completely unalike, excepting Slade's delusion of having Beth.

Three is an unpredictable and violent sector. Perhaps not as violent as One, but a less certain sector. On Sector One, everyone encountered is an enemy. That one thing is very predictable.

Slade will be safe only with Jeb's help. And Jeb isn't feeling particularly magnanimous.

"Stop," Slade says abruptly, and Jeb keeps walking, tossing a *why* over his shoulder.

"I scent a problem."

Jeb halts, and turning only halfway toward Slade, he places his right foot to rest on a knot of tree roots; the enchanted forest where they landed is no more, having given way to mundane, magic-less trees. Jeb tilts his head upward. Those trees' presence passively guards Slade from the Three's single blazing sun.

Jeb flares his nostrils, and though he scents Beth fairly well, and to a lesser extent, Gunnar and the Threes, he does not smell Ryan—or anything else of worth.

However, Jeb is Reflective, not Bloodling, and therein lies a critical difference. Jeb does not have the vampiric ancestry necessary to smell a drop of musk in a coliseum. A pure Bloodling could. In this, he must defer to Slade.

Jeb scowls.

Slade misses his opportunity to grin at what he surely thinks is a Reflective failing.

His head is tipped back, long black hair is spilling around his shoulders. Slade's lips are slightly parted, arms are flung wide—his eyes shut.

Jeb remains quiet, letting the Bloodling continue whatever he's doing.

"I smell gun oil." Slade's chin lowers, and his indifferent gaze meets Jeb's. The Bloodling's eyes are cups of shadows beneath his brow in the quickly fading light of day.

"Gun oil?" Jeb furiously attempts to recall what weapons of this era are prevalent.

Fossil fuel is being aggressively phased out in this *time* on Three, he's sure. Traditional gun rights are facing an aggressive challenge through a constitutional amendment. Jeb palms his chin. He can't recall exactly what it is.

He is not at his best with the history and accents of the Sectors. His concentration and interest are focused differently, toward justice and defense.

"What is the significance?" Jeb asks quickly.

Slade jerks his jaw back in clear surprise. "A—humanoid—"

"Three," Jeb corrects.

"It is no matter," Slade says, still narrowly searching their immediate area. "A humanoid from this planet has been cleaning a killing weapon with gun oil."

"A professional?" Jeb asks.

Slade nods. "Men who kill frequently generally take excellent care of their weapons."

That has been Jeb's experience as well. His searing gaze stays pegged on Slade. "How do you know of guns?"

Slade folds his arms, his lids lowering to half-mast. "Contraband."

"Ah," Jeb says, letting the sarcasm blow through his reply. That *would* make sense. Corrupt Sector One. Of course.

Slade's frown marks tight angles and planes across his face as he studies Jeb's expression. "You judge me, but hear this—if there are assassins close to us, close to Beth, we need to ask ourselves why." His voice is soft, but he has the unusual ability to almost throw the modulation like a ventriloquist, and Jeb catches his words easily. "If Ryan were the only obstacle in our way of returning everyone to where they hail from, then what of this?"

Jeb shakes his head, parking a hand on his thigh. After a few moments, he admits slowly, "I am not a lover of coincidence."

"Nor I," Slade adds, frowning. "I think we need something besides my good looks to get us close to Beth, without alerting this other group of our presence."

Jeb smirks, thinking Slade doesn't look that well. "No one will have the abilities of the two of us. We are on Three, a most primitive world in terms of males who can handle themselves. Many of this world's males are without worth, having nothing to back up their posturing."

"And what of the females?"

Jeb pulls an unconcerned face, lifting a dismissive shoulder and letting it drop. "They are soft."

"Beth is not, Merrick. Beth is fierce in all things."

This is true. "She is Reflective."

Slade mutters something underneath his breath.

"What did you say?" Jeb continues to look sharply at Slade.

"There are other beings that might give you concern, Jeb Merrick."

Jeb shrugs. "I don't worry about the Three's guns or their other crude, slow weaponry."

"Because you hop, eh?" Slade asks, his chin hiking, hands going to his hips.

"Yes," Jeb says, not adding the *of course* at the end of his reply. "Reflectives do not hop, they *jump*," he adds with mental disdain.

"And if you cannot hop your way out of a mess?" Slade inquires softly.

Jeb straightens, his hands fisting. "Then I fight, Bloodling."

"Ah"—he wags his finger at Jeb—"the first thing of merit you've uttered."

"I do not have time for your assumptions about Reflectives. Or what I consider myself to be, or my abilities. I have been training to be an assassin, a soldier, and a bearer of justice since the age of five cycles, and nothing will alter that directive."

"Even our fair Beth?"

Jeb whirls in the opposite direction, leaving Slade behind him.

Slade's chuckling follows him, and Jeb's veins burn with pent frustration.

Let the Threes come bearing arms or whatever battle they think they can muster.

Jeb is ready.

"Guns," Gunnar says with barely more than a breath, his nostrils flaring.

Beth doesn't move—and can't smell the guns. But her vision is just fine, and she sees them hoisted steadily in strong hands.

Ryan stays at the crest of the ravine, looking down on them like a god.

He isn't one. And Beth will not give him more of an advantage by getting near him. Besides, she can see no benefit when he is above her.

"Who are these guys?"

Government spooks, Beth answers mentally, taking inventory of their manner, wardrobe, and deliberate stealth.

"Jackson Kennedy Caldera?" calls one in the lead, though Beth doesn't see his face clearly behind the weapon he holds.

Slowly, she extracts her blade, thankful she chose the black ceramic before their journey. White would present like a flag in the shadowed forest.

"God," Jacky mutters, jabbing a thumb at his chest, his eyebrows to his hairline. "Nope. That guy's dead. Me and my buds here are taking a little stroll through the woods."

Gunnar moves in front of Maddie, and the approaching men flick their laser eyes to him.

None of them seem surprised to see a Bloodling male.

More unease buries itself in Beth, flooding her insides, and she shifts her weight, observing the five armed men. They're outfitted in the black military garb popular in Three as they zigzag a path closer to their position.

"Vamp world male, four o'clock," the lead Three says into a mic close to his face.

Vamp world—could they mean One?

"My daughter," Gunnar calls softly, and she knows he is using a frequency not detectable by the human Threes and turns to him in surprise. "Let them get close."

Beth subtly changes position, sliding a dagger behind her back and letting her right arm hang loose.

Tenseness would be more natural looking as these killers approach, but that will make them even more watchful.

The lead male's eyes move to Beth. "Butterfly bitch at noon."

Heat suffuses Beth's body, dull rage thumping its way through her vasculature.

She is not a bitch, and butterflies are sacred. Beth Jasper is a warrior of The Cause.

Beth feels a feral smile stretch her lips.

"Dimensional," the man begins, then his eyes sweep Maddie a second time, "or something, at four."

"Our liaison"—he speaks to Beth and indicates Ryan, standing like an imperious fortress at the top of the ravine—"has told us how dangerous you are. Stand down, and we won't hurt the boy and the"—he looks to Maddie again—"female," he finally decides.

Beth's sharkish grin widens.

There is nothing for Ryan to reflect to help these males—as there is nothing for her.

She senses Gunnar's readiness.

Beth speaks in the ancient language of Sector One, knowing her father will understand and the Threes will not.

Gunnar shoves Maddie down, and the men follow his motion.

"Stop!" the leader of the Threes bellows.

Gunnar disobeys, of course, and crouches, leaping with his powerful legs he flies at them.

A shot fires, blasting a hole through Gunnar's shoulder, and Beth gives a minute flinch. A gemlike spray of blood bursts from his body. Vague spears of late daylight stab through the thick tree cover, hitting the red drops.

Beth tracks them, seeing what she needs, and leaps.

The blood tastes like liquid metal as she slides through it and lands on the leader.

He doesn't have time to round his weapon to shoot her, and Beth's hand chops his throat, neatly arresting his breathing.

Dragging her dagger from behind her body with her left hand, she steadies against the forest floor with her right and sweeps the blade up at the back of the second man's thigh, severing the hamstring.

He drops, howling at the top of his lungs and clutching at his spurting leg.

Beth moves forward, cutting the throat of the third in an upward, jumping hack.

Ryan roars at the top of the hill, and she hears his thundering gait through the leaves and branches.

Soon, she thinks, chancing a glance at Gunnar.

He already has Maddie and Jacky beside him. She has just a moment of bone-jarring relief when he bellows her name.

Fear lathers her insides, and Beth turns, bringing up her blade as she does.

She makes a gash through Ryan's face, and he backhands her.

Her cheek splits open, and Beth staggers backward, keeping her blade out and wide with her left hand, gripping whatever she can with her right.

Slade's strong hand steadies her as the fourth and fifth men of Three that Ryan brought with him gun him down.

Slade's blood soaks her face, and still, he folds her against him, shielding her with his body.

Beth opens her eyes, her lashes glued shut with Slade's blood, and watches Jeb's body arc over theirs, crashing into Ryan.

The fifth male presses a scalding circle to her forehead. "Call them off, or I'll spray your brains, bitch."

Beth flattens her lips. "Kill him, Merrick."

The click of a trigger is loud in her ears.

6

Beth

Slade rolls her body when the hammer clicks on the Three's weapon at the exact moment Beth sights a sliver of polished stainless on Ryan's blackened buckle, worn away just enough.

Beth jumps them both, and the bullet meant for her brain beats into the ground she just jumped them from.

Barreling into Reflective Ryan from a meter and a half above his head, she and Slade drop hard.

Beth determines two hundred and fifty pounds of Bloodling has soundly rung Ryan's bell until his hand closes around her throat.

She brings her knee up, and he plants his on her thigh, pinning her leg and spreading it at the same time.

Principle. Beth twists her head to the right and bites his wrist, trying to meet her teeth together.

Ryan groans, tightening his hold.

Oxygen consumption stops, and stars burst in the field of her vision.

Jeb's fist slams into his temple. Ryan jerks his head back and forth, as though he'd shake off the blow.

Beth shifts her torso hard, and the sudden movement throws Ryan's balance. Lifting her upper body, she brings her blade up, skewing him in the gut. She corkscrews the serrated ceramic inside his body.

His eyes widen, and thin threads of red sink between his teeth as blood shoots up into his mouth.

"Mongrel," he manages.

Beth nods. "The mongrel who's killing you."

"Stand down, Reflective bitch."

Beth's eyes slide to the right. The single Three who Beth didn't manage to incapacitate holds Maddie, a gun pressed to her head.

Beth bares her teeth.

"Don't you fucking do that jumping shit"—he rams the tip against her temple, and Maddie's shimmering lavender-blue eyes tighten—"or I'll do her."

Beth grins. "Let her go, and I'll let you live."

He barks out a laugh, clicking the safety off. "You're in no position to negotiate."

Beth's eyes naturally seek reflection, coming to the barrel of his gun. The black of the barrel vaguely gleams.

She tracks—calculating.

At that exact moment, the sun sinks, shading everything to opaque smears, and just like that, the Reflectives are reduced to their combat and wits.

"Get up," he says and shakes Maddie, who yelps at the treatment.

Beth dare not look around her.

Is Gunnar unharmed? *Slade?*

Jeb stands beside her.

She rolls a bleeding Ryan off and stands, wasting a glance on his writhing form. Even as she looks, his hands close around the hilt and jerk her dagger from his body. Beth kicks it from his hand.

Fresh blood slowly pools from the wound she just inflicted. Ryan is Reflective and will heal even this grievous of an injury unless she finishes him.

"Scoot your ass topside." His eyes move to Jeb. "You too, pretty boy."

Jeb's eyes narrow, and he moves slightly in front of Beth, which makes her angry. "Let us go, and no harm will come to you."

Beth rolls her eyes. Speak *Three,* Jeb.

The Three snorts, but his cool eyes remain on her partner. "No. Can. Do." His eyes scan behind him, and he notices something. "As you were, big guy, or the girl gets a permanent dirt nap."

Gunnar. Beth senses him. Then he hisses, and she knows.

"Grab your buddy and haul his fanged ass topside too." He snorts, his grip tightening on Maddie severely. "Need to muzzle him. Already bled out two of my men."

Healing the bullet wounds. Took his pound of flesh—or liter of blood. Beth's lips lift, and she flicks her eyes at Gunnar. Only a vague scar remains where the bullet passed through him.

The Bloodlings repair even faster than Reflectives. Now Beth knows why she is the fastest healing Reflective in The Cause. Part Bloodling. They'd certainly never credited the reason as her being female.

Beth's exhale is frustrated. Ryan's been saved by the corrupt Threes, who have imprisoned them.

The Three toes Ryan as he groans on the damp moss. "He gonna live?"

Beth gives a grim nod. "Oh yes."

He shakes his head in wonder. "Amazing as fuck."

Jeb's eyes tighten, ignoring the Three's crude summation. "Where are we going?"

"Wherever I feel like." The Three is hard, but Beth knows Jeb is harder.

Then he slams the butt of the gun into Jeb's stomach. Jeb staggers forward but doesn't make a sound.

Beth moves to strike, and he levels the pistol in her face.

"Stand down, sweetheart."

Beth's heart jams up her throat as the Three's eyes dare her to try him.

She wants to, badly.

"Beth," Jeb says softly, straightening with a wince.

"Welcome to earth," Jacky mutters, and Beth's shoulders tense with the butt-shaped bruise of a gun on his face. He sees her notice. "Eff it, it's all the guy got in." He grins.

Beth's pride in the boy swells. He's brash and irritating but has a good heart.

"We don't need you, kid. You're expendable."

Jacky's eyes train on him. "Doubt it. You couldn't find your ass with both hands, judging by how all your guys got their clocks cleaned."

The Three scowls, jerking his head toward the top of the ravine. "Get your asses up there. Move!"

Jacky gives him a last glare and shimmies up the ravine toward the back of his ruined domicile.

Jeb and Beth move together, making the climb easily, Slade and Gunnar at their backs.

Beth can feel the gaze of the Three boring into her back as she keeps every intuitive sense at the ready, in case some escape presents itself.

They reach the top, where unmarked cars in sleek jet-black are parked along the curb. Clean exhaust spirals up toward the night sky, where stars are just beginning to show against the midnight-blue blanket of night.

"We jump at first reflection," Jeb says in quiet Latin.

Then he stumbles forward, hitting the ground hard with his palms.

Blood pools in a gash at the back of his head, and Beth pivots. The gun rounds at her a second time, and she leans back on her tiptoes in avoidance, her arms thrown wide for balance. The blow glances on her chin and takes her back a step where she rocks to flat-footed and balances.

"No!" Beth shouts as Maddie throws a surprise punch at the Three who struck him in the crotch.

He goes down, and she kicks his gun away. It spins on what's survived of the driveway.

Car doors open, and silent Threes exit their vehicles. "Stop now, or we gun you down. All of you."

Jeb stands, his wound already beginning to clot.

Beth tenses in readiness.

"No, Beth."

She glances at Jeb.

Beth swims through the sick adrenaline pumping through her body. She can identify when a male has potential she has to address.

The Three who just spoke is one who has it.

She and Jeb face the new threat. "Go ahead. Fucking go for it. Doesn't matter to me either way. I get paid by the hour."

"Union fuckwit," Jacky grumbles.

His hard gaze moves to the youngling. "You especially. You think I won't kill a kid?" His laugh sounds like broken glass to Beth's ears. He yanks his jaw to the Threes who flank him. "I *so* will."

Jacky says nothing, thank Principle.

His eyes quickly scan her and Jeb then move to behind him. "Hey, Keith, what in the fuck are these?" His flinty attention is behind her. Beth doesn't need to turn around to know he's asking about the Bloodlings.

"Vamps," the Three who struck Jeb in the back of the head gasps from the ground, where he's attempting to relearn how to breathe.

"Get the kids."

Jeb tenses, and it is Beth who grabs his arm.

The head Three lifts his chin. "You a slow learner, Reflective?"

He says Reflective like *dolt*.

The men engage in a weighted stare.

Beth wants his death, and judging by Jeb's expression, he feels the same.

The Three must see the intent in their expressions, and they smile slowly. "I bet you two would like to take us out. But that's not going to happen. Keith's going to get his nuts in a sack and help remove the bodies from the ravine."

Keith chooses that opportunity to throw up.

Jeb's smirk is immediate—satisfied.

The other Three laughs. "As soon as he stops upchucking."

Beth and Jeb don't join in. She doesn't think their situation is funny. She doesn't even have to wonder if Jeb is scheming. She knows he is.

The Threes walk cautiously by them, and Beth doesn't even look at the man who told them to get Jacky and Maddie.

He has them within the sights of his weapon. It's black as pitch here, and there is no reflection. Her chest grows tight as she realizes Ryan is alive and he will exact vengeance.

She made a grave error in judgment. Beth should have waited for Slade and Jeb.

He lifts his chin. "Shoot the vamps."

"No!" Beth whirls, launching behind herself.

Jeb misses grabbing her.

Slade's eyes meet hers. His tender gaze is on her, his body hard.

His form is peppered with the wounds he suffered, his naturally pearl-gray skin ashen.

An arrow hits his chest, and one second before she understands the Threes meant to tranquilize the Bloodlings, Beth feels the bite in her own shoulder.

Reflectives metabolize drugs rapidly, so the drugs will not be as effective.

Keith moves toward her, and she roundhouse kicks him in the teeth, a martial arts technique she studied that's prevalent on Three.

He falls backward, and a single tooth falls out of his mouth, rolling off his chest to fall into his open palm.

Gunnar drops to his knees, his longish black hair uncoiled from his hair club.

A man falls on her back, and Beth's vision wavers.

Principle no. She bends, upending him over the top of her.

Jeb fights behind her, and a gunshot rings in her ears.

"The shit's not working!"

"It shall," Ryan says from beside her. He holds his guts, and with a stiff knuckle jab, Beth strikes him hard at the site of the wound.

He folds but manages to grab her wrist on the way down.

Nausea rolls through her as she twists her wrist hard in the opposite direction of his hold.

His grip tightens.

They stare at each other for a heartbeat, then Ryan straightens, and she pulls back. He keeps the vice grip on her wrist, and Beth strikes him in the nose with the front of her free hand.

But her precision is skewed, and where she thought his nose was, there is only air as her hand passes harmlessly by his head.

Her vision narrows to gray at the edges as a roaring sound fills her ears.

Ryan bashes his closed fist into her cheek, and she sags.

"Beth!" Jeb roars.

Ryan holds her aloft by one arm cranked behind her. "Stay down, Jasper," he grits from between his teeth.

She cranes her neck to look up at him, but there are three Ryans instead of one. "Never."

He nods as though he expected that response.

When he hits her again, she can't stay awake.

7

Beth

Beth comes awake in broken chunks of consciousness and pain. She carefully moves her jaw from side to side and winces at the stiffness.

The floor beneath her feels cool, and she rolls to her side, her eyes still shut, and presses a forearm to the ground. After a few moments, she heaves onto her forearms and knees, bowing forward as if praying.

Beth doesn't pray; she kneels because she can't stand.

Waves of dizziness undulate through her body like a slithering snake in motion. She gulps, and the urge to throw up slowly passes. Sometimes, a head injury will feel better with a good evacuation of everything from the body.

Not this time. Beth knows from experience that if she can just ride this wave of injury through, she'll mend.

She lets the knowledge of the condition she's in fade away from her brain. She also disallows the shakes from lack of food and water.

Beth is Reflective and trained to eschew basic needs. There are other matters more important than the temporary setback of being imprisoned by corrupt Threes, guided by the even more criminal intent of Reflective Lance Ryan.

Thinking of him makes her angry, breathing new life into her psyche. Beth lifts her head just enough from between her flattened palms, keeping herself centered, breaths even and deep, and scans her surroundings.

Bars of a soft gray surround her at every turn. Beth hoists herself on her rear and surveys the environment.

She's inside a prison of sorts with bars of ceramic-coated stainless steel, which tells Beth that the Threes, or Ryan, have already anticipated housing Reflectives. Her stomach begins to churn anew. Premeditation is wholly different than Threes just stumbling upon their little party and making an opportunistic capture.

She tilts her head upward, studying the roof of the same material as the bars. She turns her attention to the floor, and her heartbeats accelerate. Her gaze shifts to what looks like cement beneath her. Certain regions of the Greater Quadrant of America may still use granite flakes within the manufacture of this material.

Her eyes flick to the other cells' flooring. She sees nothing. Beth stiffens her shoulders. Something will present itself for her to jump.

Blinking rapidly, Beth staggers over a sight she hoped never to see.

Jeb is tied down within his cell.

Four ceramic-coated stainless rings are driven into the corners of the square holding pen, and some type of plastic ropes anchor his wrists and ankles, which are spread away from his torso.

Zip ties, Beth suddenly remembers.

Beth's breath releases in an anguished rush. The Bloodlings have trap doors above the roofs of their cells.

Sunlight. Beth shudders.

Maddie and Jacky are together in one cell and appear to be sleeping. Or drugged. Beth can't discount what might have transpired after she was beaten into unconsciousness.

Her eyes travel back to Slade and Gunnar's cells. Beth understands on some level that they're all being held like animals.

Jeb groans, startling Beth out of her reverie. She walks over to the side of her cell, wraps her chilled fingers around the bars, and looks directly into his. Her eyes run the distance between them and estimate that about three meters separate their holding pens.

Jeb turns his face, his eyes catching hers.

Beth blinks back her emotions, and a thought occurs to her, and she searches the four corners of her own cell. Rings stand in nonreflective repose. Just seeing the benign anchors speeds her heart.

"Beth," Jeb rasps.

She turns back to him, sees his vulnerability, and the urge to cry anew is brutal resistance clogging her airway. Tears are a luxury, one she can't afford. "Merrick," she finally croaks.

His look is bold, possessive. "They think I am the threat, so I've been…" He lifts his hands, and the ties snap with the tension.

"But you're not the only threat," she says quietly.

He shakes his head. "No."

"Do whatever you need to survive, Beth. Do it for me." His Adam's apple bobs with his swallow, and Beth sees Jeb is fighting the horrible emotions of a bonded male. A man who has found his soul mate. His eyes won't release her, and she feels imprisoned by his command.

"And me."

Beth's attention swings to the new voice.

Slade grabs the smooth bars of his cell as his black eyes find her in the dim lighting of the space.

"Slade," Beth begins, dipping her chin, "I'm afraid—"

"—you would be a fool not to be."

Beth shakes her head, and loose hair falls in front of her aching, abraded face. "I am not afraid."

"Let me guess, you're Reflective," Jacky says from his cell. His voice is poisonous with disdain.

Beth levels her eyes on him. "That's correct. But further, fear will rob me of everything I can bring to help us."

"You're not speaking like a Three, Beth," Jeb says softly.

The backs of her eyelids burn, her throat tightening further. "No," she concedes in a whisper.

"Daughter," Gunnar calls softly.

The emotion in his voice is insistent velvet against her, and Beth bites the inside of her cheek to rein in her chaotic emotions.

She slowly turns her face in his direction.

"What are these Threes like? What chances do we have against them?"

Beth grips the bars, her eyes scanning their surroundings more closely for a second time. She is so attuned to anything that holds reflective properties that sensing them is not uncommon. Her eyes sweep back to Gunnar.

"I—without anything to reflect from—I can't jump." She indicates the floor beneath with a palm. "If this were true recycled material, there'd be a chance it would retain granite from its manufacture."

"It doesn't have any because we need that stone for other stuff, like houses. Not cement. Wasteful," Jacky sings in the background.

Beth's hands tighten on the bars. "Those small flakes are reflective."

"What are we going to do?" Maddie asks quietly.

I'm not sure.

Beth switches to Three speech. "We'll see what they're going to do with us. With Ryan in the mix, anything can happen. He's an unpredictable male."

"He's not a real Reflective. He's a dissenter," Jeb growls from the floor.

"True, Merrick," Slade agrees.

Gunnar waves their words away. "We already understand what Ryan is. I heard about the illegal games of Reflectives pitted against one another for blood sport." His flat black gaze moves to Beth. "Let's come up with some kind of plan. Something for now."

"The plan is, we kick these guys' asses and get the hell out of dodge."

Beth almost smiles. Almost.

"We need to get out of here, that much is true. Then we need to jump to One and try to reacquire Rachett."

Slade tilts his head, and a fine strand of ebony hair falls forward, gently curving around his jaw. "Beth, I told you—"

"—I don't care. Merrick and I can't leave him there. If Ratchett's dead, so be it, but the least we can do is exhaust that he might not be."

"Dangerous," Jacky comments in a bald voice, leaning against the bars, his arms folded.

Beth turns, her humor gone. "Yes. Everything we do is dangerous. It is our lives."

"But not ours, Jasper. Me and Mad"—he jerks a thumb at Maddie—"we just want to stay here and figure it out. I mean, once we kick their asses."

Thirteen cycles, Beth reminds herself.

"Jacky, you will never be safe here. Your parents and home are no more." She plows forward, regardless of the numb expression overtaking his face. Some words must be said, no matter how horrible to utter. "Jeb and I—Reflective Merrick," she pauses, dipping her chin. *I will not hide.* She scrapes the insides of herself for fortitude. Raising her eyes, she meets his. "We will do what we can to provide a home of some kind for you both on Papilio."

"Pfft!" Jacky kicks a bar. "What Papilio? The effed mess of Reflective women whores and Reflectives that don't know how to put shit back together?"

"Jacky," Maddie begins, "they're trying—"

"Nah. I get it, Mad." Jacky's eyes stare at Beth, then move to Merrick as he cranes his neck backward to meet Jacky's infuriated gaze. "You guys are doing your best, but I'm thinking my best might be better. Maybe I just avoid all of ya, and then I won't be like—collateral damage or some shit."

Beth blinks. She hates what the youngling says, but from his perspective, it might be very true. Maybe he and Maddie *are* safer without being around Reflectives.

Her eyes sweep the holding cells, finding no weakness in construction—nothing to jump from. Her attention shifts to a vaulted ceiling, all dulled metal. Open-ceiling rafters with pulse-on lighting in LED shine softly down at them. Enough for illumination but not enough to see very well by.

Who is she to say that they will protect him and Maddie when they're currently imprisoned by his own people?

"You're an ungrateful youngling," Slade comments.

Jacky tilts his head back, his eyes like bright slivers of emeralds on Slade. "Yeah, you just figured that? Well, news flash, fangface, I dig Merrick and Jasper. I know a lot of shit that's come down isn't their fault. Those are the facts, man. But"—he points at Slade—"shit *still* came down, and we're covered in it."

"Jacky's right," Jeb concedes quietly.

Jacky chuckles. "Now I *know* crap's bad if Merrick agrees with anything I say."

Jeb snorts. "Yes, now is definitely not the time for optimism."

"This solves nothing. My kindred blood is held prisoner, and I can't defend her." Gunnar wraps his strong hands around the bars, his naturally gray flesh bleeding to white from the tension. He and Maddie stare at each other.

Jacky mimes fangs with his fingers inside his open mouth. "And do some blood suck, huh?"

Gunnar glares at Jacky.

Maddie giggles, and Gunnar frowns.

"You Bloodling dudes are seriously without humor. *Not* a good trait."

The door opens, and the group collectively stiffens, moving back to the center of their cells.

Jeb whistles in a frequency a Three couldn't detect; twenty-five thousand hertz.

Beth strides back to the part of her cell nearest him.

"Remember what I said. They expect less from you." Using their native Latin is a risk. Jeb was beaten with the stock of a gun for speaking it before.

Of course, Ryan understands Latin perfectly, but he's not the man who walks through the door.

"Hello, folks." He smiles, and Beth backs away from the bars, keeping her arms loose and at her sides.

A Three male, one of about forty-three cycles, strolls casually between the cells. He wears a white lab coat and stands nearly six feet. Beth hisses an inhale when she senses his IQ.

Jeb and she make eye contact. One hundred eighty. Scientist.

She smiles reassuringly at Jeb. This Three cannot fight. He doesn't carry himself as though he is familiar with his body's limitations. That gives the Reflectives an immediate advantage.

"I'm Carl Lindstrom, and I'm in charge of this study."

"I'm an American. I have rights," Jacky fires back.

Lindstrom gives Jacky his sharp attention. "Not here. You're under what our loophole-filled government coins as *need*." With curved fingertips, he makes quotes around the last word.

"Bullshit. My parents and house are gone. I'm nothing special. I'm not needed for dick, Einstein."

His face wrinkles in distaste. "You don't have paranormal talent. Yet." He runs a finger down his pulse device. "Jackson Caldera." Lindstrom lifts his face, smiling happily.

Jacky raises his middle finger. "Sit and spin, douche."

"Ah yes, the poetry of our foul youth." His eyes narrow on Jacky, who scowls defiantly back.

Lindstrom returns his attention to her and Jeb. "You've been sloppy, getting caught with your collective underwear down." He makes a tsk-tsk noise. "Lance had mentioned that Reflective Merrick had some innate timepiece, and its function is some kind of biological directive to become aware of the perfect mate?" Lindstrom belly laughs, giving a small shake of his head. "As you might already be aware, I am a scientist, and as such, I hold little faith in anything that is not tangible. So without further ado, myself and Lance Ryan will begin the fun." He rubs his hands together as though he's a caricature of an evil villain.

"What are you talking about?" Beth speaks for the first time.

"The experimentation, of course. We finally have the Bloodlings and Reflectives? Excellent." His smile broadens. "If the males resist full cooperation with my tests, I will harm the women."

"And you will die," Slade states blandly, an unhealthy sheen coating his skin. At least his many bullet wounds have closed.

"With great slowness," Gunnar adds.

Beth sighs. The Bloodlings are very focused but not always the best strategists when females are threatened.

"Very well," Lindstrom replies. "I'm counting on that kind of intensity." His eyes glitter mercilessly on Jeb.

"We begin with you."

Beth grips the rails, pressing her face between the bars so tightly it stretches the skin of her face taut. "We have Directives of The Cause, Carl Lindstrom."

He turns his head, inspecting her as though she were an interesting bug. "That may be. However, your code of ethics is not nearly as entertaining as seeing what kind of damage Reflective Merrick can heal. And that is only the proverbial tip of the learning iceberg."

Beth stares at him for a full minute.

He finally drops his eyes, and Beth knows she'll break the sixth directive first:

Take life only in defense of another.

8

Merrick

A smugly repulsive Lance Ryan strolls in after the scientist's self-congratulatory spiel.

Jeb tenses.

There's nothing he can do short of sawing off his hands—for now. He stays where he lies.

Jeb's eyes slowly drift over his immediate surroundings for the hundredth time. There is not a flake of reflection, grain of sand—nothing. Every surface is dull and without shine. He's certain Beth has made the same perusal.

"Don't bother," Ryan says in Three lingo with a dismissive sneer. "I have thoroughly vetted the area, and it's without reflection."

Jeb lifts his head off the cell's quartz floor and watches Ryan's catlike walk as he moves with graceful purpose from one cell to the next.

His lips flatten as Ryan pauses in front of Maddie and Jacky's cell. Jacky slowly lifts his middle finger in a well-established Three gesture of crudity that Jeb recalls roughly means *get fucked* or something along those lines.

Ryan's laugh bursts from between his lips. "You're ballsy for a Three. You know I could crush you, yet you continue to defy at every turn."

Jacky shrugs, raising his arm a bit higher while maintaining the stiff middle finger.

Ryan's attention shifts to Madeline, and she shrinks against the bars. "You didn't hurt me before," she says in a subdued voice.

Gunnar growls, shaking the bars that hold him.

Ryan nods slowly. "That's true." He shifts his gaze to Gunnar, bestowing a cruel smile on the Bloodling.

Maddie comes away from the bars, moving closer to Ryan. "Then let me and Jacky go. I don't want the others hurt, but…" Maddie bites her lip and doesn't continue.

Jeb shuts his eyes. He can almost predict, word for word, how the debauched Reflective will answer. And he does not disappoint.

"Somehow, you evaded our notice for the five years you were in Papilio."

Jeb twists his aching neck around to watch the exchange. He can do nothing, yet he can't look away, can't hide the scene unfolding from his sight.

"Do not touch her, hopper," Gunnar warns. His voice is smooth. It would be difficult to hear the threat if one was not expressly listening for it.

Jeb always is.

Ryan's smile is tight. "Fuck off, as the Threes would say."

"I will bleed you dry—again." The sides of his lips twitch. "The only place you will hop will be inside your own grave."

Ryan pivots, facing Gunnar.

The males regard each other, neither blinking.

"You are a great warrior on One. You might be again. If you play your cards right, Bloodling."

Gunnar frowns.

Jeb scowls. This was not what he expected, and he quickly translates the Three slang: Gunnar must cooperate, and the potential for freedom awaits.

Ryan slowly turns to face Maddie again. "How?"

She swallows. "I saw what the Reflectives were doing to the women, and I didn't, I won't be used like that." Her reply is more an evasion than answer.

Ryan stares at Maddie, the silence swelling until he bellows, "How?" The veins stand out on his forehead, pulsing with anger.

Maddie jumps, quickly shaking her head as she clasps her hands tightly together. "I'm not going to say." Jacky stands, coming to her side. Though he offers no protection, he has a lion's heart.

Jeb's shoulders ease, his neck screaming for him to rest his head on the hard floor. That would have been terrible had Ryan gone to Beth's domicile and found Maddie sequestered.

THE REFLECTIVE DISSENT

"Fine. Avoid my question of your secret hiding place. But you will not go anywhere. You will answer my questions—and you *will* become my mate."

The collective inhales, Jeb's included, howl like wind in the room.

"She is my kindred blood, hopper."

Ryan snaps his head in Gunnar's direction. His eyes are angry razors of azure hate. "Excellent. Let's duel. That's customary on One." Ryan lifts a shoulder, bracing his arms together with his fingers curled around his massive biceps.

Gunnar gives a curt nod then adds, "*Without* reflection, hopper."

"You may call me Ryan or Reflective. But hopper is a little…I don't know"—his eyebrows slowly rise—"like ringing the dinner bell for your own extermination."

"He's not a bug, dickbag," Jacky says, an eyebrow cocked.

Ryan whirls, his hand sliding between the bars and snatching Jacky's arm before two blinks of an eye.

Maddie lurches forward to help, and Beth screams the boy's name.

He yanks Jacky forward, Jacky's face smacking into the bars like tenderized meat.

Jeb hears the snap of bone and the youngling's bellow.

He can just make out Jacky's sag with his peripheral vision as the boy slides down the bars, and Maddie grabs him from behind.

Ryan makes an elaborate show of releasing him by throwing up his hands, and Jacky falls backward, moaning.

"Now *that* was satisfying," Ryan says.

"You are without honor," Slade remarks, looking from the boy to the Reflective with clear disgust.

"Sadly for you, yes. Now, let's move forward."

"No!" Maddie cries from the ground where she holds Jacky. "You can't leave him like this. He'll *die*."

Ryan appears to study the spot where a jagged bone juts out of Jacky's upper arm. "He'll live. But I don't give a shit either way." A flutter appears in his jaw. "I know that he needed to be taught a long-overdue lesson, and it worked beautifully. He's now in too much pain to be an irritant."

"Been," Jacky gasps, "holdin' out on ya"—he chokes, gritting his teeth—"dickhead."

Jeb jerks his body further, trying in vain to see better.

"I hate you now," Maddie admits in a voice gone low with hate. Her cheeks shine with tears. "You hurt the only family I've got left."

Ryan smiles, ignoring Jacky. "*I* will be your family. No one else will matter once we're mated. Especially this sad excuse of a youngling." His eyes slide to Gunnar. "Or a washed-up Bloodling."

Gunnar's fingers curl the bar, and Jeb swears he can hear them creak from the pressure.

Jacky smiles, and Jeb's shock washes over him. Ryan would not wait until his timepiece disintegrated? He would take a young woman, barely more than a youngling, for a life partner just because he can? Of course, Ryan is capable of all things vile. That much is proven. Jeb knows through tough, recent experience that once a soul mate is located, one is helpless against the pull. Ryan would be a horrible mate to anyone. Possibly even his destined one.

"Scratch your ass, monkey boy," Jacky says tersely, breathing through his pain and shattering Jeb's train of thought.

Jeb's jaw drops. *What in Principle's name is he up to?* Does Jacky want to suffer more abuse? Because he's damn sure Ryan will mete it.

For a moment, Ryan looks confused. Then, amazingly, he complies.

Jeb blinks, certain he's seeing a mirage. But *no*. Ryan reaches around and begins clawing at his right buttocks.

A laugh bursts out from someone, but Ryan doesn't notice. He's busy doing what Jacky said.

Amazing.

"Lift me up, Mad."

Maddie jerks Jacky up by the armpits, and they heave backward together. The Three is small enough with the age regression that occurred that she doesn't have to work too much, but the boy seems to be breathing through his anguish.

Lindstrom apparently recovers from his shock and begins running to Ryan.

Jacky casts a sardonic glance toward the scientist, his lips twisting. "Trip over your own feet, Carl."

Midstride, the scientist makes a deliberate twisting motion with one foot and belts forward, catching himself with his palms from a bruising landing at the last minute.

"Manipulator," Maddie says quietly, almost to herself.

Jacky adjusts his position, his skin beginning to pale from shock. "Yup. I could feel the compulsion to tell these asshats what to do and *bam*—look at how good that shit turned out."

Ryan's expression is pained. However, he keeps scratching.

Jeb's lips quirk.

Jacky snorts then groans. "This fucking hurts, but it's been great to see Ryan digging a hole to China through his pants. *Nicccce.*"

"Jacky." Beth's voice reaches Jeb, and she flicks her eyes to him as their eyes meet then return to Jacky. "I know you're hurting, but can you, like, free us?"

Jacky stares at her, and Jeb holds his breath. Thirteen cycles is terribly immature to make tough decisions. Especially when the boy's personality is mixed into the equation—and the broken arm.

"Duh. I never wanted to *not* help out, I just don't want to hang with any of you danger magnets anymore. Shortens the lifespan."

"Reflective Ryan," Jacky smirks, obviously gaining control of his mischievous glee, "stop itching your ass and pulse all these cells open and free my friends."

"No," Ryan says, still working over his posterior, a scowl firmly affixed to his face.

Jacky's face screws up in a look of pinched concentration. "Do it."

Ryan's face ripples in agony, and he slaps his hands over his head, obviously trying to shake off the compulsion. With jerky, robotic movements, he moves to the first cell that holds Jeb.

Their eyes meet.

"No." Ryan grits his teeth.

"I'm gonna turn up the mojo, assjack. So *do it*."

"No!" Carl bellows from the ground.

"You"—Jacky points with a shaking finger—"shut your piehole."

Lindstrom does, his teeth snapping together with a click.

Ryan lifts his thumb slowly and presses Jeb's cell.

Jeb doesn't want to break whatever magical thrall Jacky's somehow managed. Nor does he question the *why* of how this has all transpired. That can come later, when they're well past this challenge.

He simply waits for opportunity to present itself. Jeb has found temperance to be an acquired taste.

Ryan staggers inside the cell, as though each step costs a piece of him.

Probably, for Ryan, it does.

Their eyes meet across the speckled flooring, and Ryan breathes through his nose in big, sucking inhales, as if he's suffocating on his own breaths.

"Control your breathing, or you'll hyperventilate," Jacky says.

Ryan immediately complies, his expression pinched. He walks reluctantly to Jeb, dumping to the floor, where he lands hard on his knees, and with a ceramic blade, he cuts through the plastic ties.

He then knee-walks to all four corners and repeats the same to each ankle, each wrist.

Jeb rises with his torso first, not moving quickly. Feeling returns in a painful surge to his extremities and lastly to his ass, partially deadened from lying for hours on the unforgiving floor.

Ryan's hands clench and unclench into fists as he helplessly watches Jeb gain freedom.

Jeb stands, stretching to the ceiling of the barred pen, and every bone in his spine pops from the motion.

A Three would have a massive headache from the drug the Threes employed to force them into the unnatural sleep they found themselves in. However, a Reflective has a different metabolism and healing capacity.

Jeb has rid himself of both the headache and is largely healed from his most recent injuries. And it's cost him. He needs fuel. Badly.

He begins to walk away from Ryan, then a thought occurs to him and he retraces his steps.

Ryan's eyes go wide as he sits on his knees, blinking rapidly. No new directive from Jacky to replace the old.

"Merrick?" Jacky says, his voice a bit panicked. "What are ya doin'?"

Jeb doesn't answer.

He takes the stout ceramic blade from Ryan's unresisting fingers and forces his hand flat on the smooth recycled flooring. All five fingers spread and tautly flat against the cold surface.

Their eyes meet.

Jeb remembers Beth's face, the bruising and the skin scraped from her knuckles. "This is for harming my soul mate."

"No, Merrick," Beth whispers.

"Yes."

Jeb brings the blade down in a swift, expert stroke and cuts off Reflective Ryan's thumb.

Ryan howls.

Jacky says, "Be quiet, Ryan."

Ryan's mouth snaps shut, and tears leak out of his eyes. Jeb understands pain has to escape somehow.

He stands, holding Reflective Ryan's warm stub of bleeding flesh between his fingers.

"Merrick, I didn't think ya had it in you," Jacky says in a squeezed-down voice of admiration.

Jeb notices Ryan's eyes are tight with his pain. The boy will need a healer. He gives a tight smile. "He'll heal." Jeb isn't sure what newfound talent the boy's come up with or why, only that it can be used to get them out of here.

Maddie looks on with horror while Jeb gives a curt nod at Jacky. "Get Lindstrom in there with Ryan."

Jacky instructs the scientist.

He walks into the cell, and as soon as he crosses the threshold, Jeb slams the door shut. The bars make a final, clanking sound, as though resisting the action.

Jeb turns Ryan's thumb and depresses the whirls of his fingerprint against the pulse dock and *thinks* it locked.

The lock engages. The thumbprint is enough. Jeb was sure it would work. After all, he and Beth had sold counterfeit disintegrating thumb skins to work their agenda with the Zondorae brothers on one of their very first assignments together.

Jeb turns, strides to Beth's cell first, and rolls the thumb over the dock once more.

The door on her cell is automatic and whispers open.

Beth looks up at him.

Neither moves.

Tension slides out of Jeb, and he moves forward, pulling his soul mate into his arms. Everything feels right and perfect—whole again. Jeb buries his face in her undone and scattered hair, her braids long gone, and breathes in her scent, relief flooding his system like a wave of endorphins. He braces his hands on either side of her face and kisses the dirt away.

She breaks away, gasping but smiling.

Jeb's face aches with his own grin.

Then Slade shatters everything like a hammer to glass. "Free us, hopper," he says in a voice that's sand in the desert.

Beth retreats from their embrace, but her smile is bright.

Jeb takes her hand and tows her to Jacky's cell and Slade's, then Gunnar's, repeating the process with Ryan's thumb.

Finally they move to where Ryan's lying, his stub still bleeding.

Soon it will clot. He's not an octopus, and he can't grow a new digit, but he can do something with the original.

Jeb chucks the thumb inside the cell, and it rolls toward the two men, and without a word, the group moves out of the room, locking the door that leads out to the main hall in the good old-fashioned way.

9

Slade

Slade slays Merrick with his eyes.

He strides around, touching Tiny Frog at every opportunity, and all Slade can think about is ways for him to die.

The Reflective is honorable. But honor does not negate blood ties.

And that is what Slade has for Beth Jasper.

Bloodlings mate for the strongest lines or position within their communities of the forests of One.

Kindred blood is such an ancient legend that's hardly ever realized. Before Gunnar, Slade can't think of an instance where he actually knew of another Bloodling who consummated such a union.

Now Slade wonders if the pairing must be between a female and male of mixed genetics. Beth is not fully Bloodling.

Madeline is not at all. Yet Gunnar says she is his Kindred Blood—as was Beth's mother.

Perhaps it is nature's design for the race remaining diverse and to keep interbreeding at a level that does not weaken but strengthens the Bloodlings.

Bloodling males do not share their mates.

Jeb Merrick will not share Beth.

What Slade wishes to know is when her timepiece is no more, who will she seek as mate?

Jeb?

Me.

Or someone else entirely, for there are many sectors.

Slade's hands clench into fists, and at just that moment, a stinging pain fires off at the base of his skull. Absently, he strokes his nape, thinking he's not been right since that last jump with Merrick.

"What about a healer for Jacky?" Beth asks from between him and Merrick.

Merrick gives her a tender glance that causes consumed blood to boil inside his gut.

Speaking of which. Slade turns behind him, briefly counting the inept Threes who guarded the door.

Their bodies stove up the open doorway like buried sardines.

A good sight, Slade muses.

He and Gunnar drank their fill in full view of the scientist and Ryan. It was a pleasure.

But now all that warm Three blood curdles as though Slade drank spoiled milk, whereas it would taste sweet—as all spoils of war do.

Slade's knowledge of his feelings for Beth—no, his instinctual compulsion to be with her—has made him testy.

His lips lift. What an understatement, as the Threes would say. And what a ruthlessly difficult language to understand. All the quadrants have different regional dialects, from what Beth says. And many of them constantly talk in strange vernacular and slang that *they* understand but that leaves Slade baffled. Especially the youngling.

Gunnar grunts ascent at Beth's comment, not in the least winded from carrying the youngling.

"A jump to Papilio will right Jacky."

Jacky groans as he shifts within Gunnar's hold. "Don't want to go back to butterfly hell, thanks."

Merrick turns with a grim set to his mouth, and Slade swings his palm up. "It appears as though everything you say incenses the boy." Slade's eyebrows pointedly rise.

Merrick glares. "And *you* would have us coddle him."

Slade shakes his head. "No. He is no one's responsibility. Let him remain here on Three." Slade turns a wide grin Jacky's way, his fangs lengthening. "I am sure, at your age, there are"—Slade swings his palm around—"protocols in place which protect the young until they become of age."

Jacky scowls.

Now we are getting somewhere.

Slade finds the boy to be exasperating yet bravely fashioned. In addition, the female that brings his blood to heal, loves him. Beth has not said so, but it's contained within the expression she wears when she gazes upon him.

Slade will manipulate his cooperation.

"No, Slade," Beth begins as though on perfect cue.

Slade smiles.

"He can't be left to his own devices. They'll ask questions, and how do we know who will tend Jacky?"

Jacky rolls his eyes, but Slade is expert on evaluating subtle emotion. And where that might fail, there is his keen Bloodling sense of smell.

Jacky wishes to be liked and cared about. He has no parents. His only brother is dead. The girl his brother loved is now the Kindred Blood of Beth's rediscovered sire.

Where does Jacky belong in the scheme of things? Slade's intuition tells him that Jacky's bravado is a clever mask of *wishing* to belong somewhere but not wanting to admit the desire.

"We'll go into the lower Kent Quadrant and find a locator, jump our group back to Papilio. Jacky's injury should heal during the jump." Merrick hikes his jaw as though the matter has already been decided.

"Wait a sec?" Maddie asks, stopping beside Gunnar. "Doesn't his break need to be set or something?"

The girl puts a strand of fine dark hair behind her ear and swings a palm up.

She is not beautiful by the narrow Reflective standards of light eyes and hair, but she is fetching in her own way. Slade has found beauty to be a multifaceted thing. Even more so since meeting Beth.

Gunnar's eyes are never off Maddie for very long.

"Whatever we're gonna do, let's do it. I feel like I'm going to hurl."

Gunnar frowns.

Slade chuckles. "He's going to vomit is what he means."

"Ah." He tips his head back in understanding. "I would prefer it if you didn't expunge the contents of your stomach on *me*."

A laugh bursts out of Maddie, and she slaps a hand over her mouth when Gunnar slides a curious glance her way.

Jacky jerks his chin back. "You sit around with a broken arm and see how good your gut feels, Big Fang."

Slade vividly remembers the manacles buried at Gunnar's ankles from the jump they took together from their home world. Something he's certain Jacky would not survive without passing out.

Gunnar doesn't appear to know what to do with the youngling's words. Is he being insulting? he clearly wonders.

In the end, Slade determines it is Jacky being Jacky.

"Jacky." Maddie turns to him, and for the first time, Slade notices how filthy they and their clothes are. There were more pressing matters to steal his attention before.

Slade's tunic is full of the blood he's drunk—and the blood of his kills. The essence of others has dried in the fine cracks of his leather tunic and now stains the garment with fissures of rust. Yet his stomach still churns.

Gunnar appears much the same, and though Beth and Maddie used the cleanser at Beth's domicile before the pursuit of the Reflectives, the hair of both females has come undone from the ornate braids Beth fashioned for them.

Bloodlings can eat food, but blood is far more easily digested. Slade and Gunnar are full. However, Slade can sense Beth's hunger though she's said nothing. *Hunger is always secondary to freedom*, Slade thinks. However, the basic need reasserts itself now that liberty has been assured.

"I like what Merrick proposes, but the females need food."

Merrick bares his teeth at Slade. "I would feed Beth if she asked."

Beth pulls a face of pure irritation, and Slade keeps his glee at bay by a thread. He enjoys usurping Merrick's attempts at romance. He's such a clod in that regard that it's a form of free entertainment.

Slade lifts a casual shoulder, turning a direct stare at Merrick. "I sense her hunger, as I sense yours. I am Bloodling. We are acutely aware of our own physical needs and those who are around us." Slade curls a fist in front of his mouth, stifling a cough.

"True," Gunnar says, his eyes roaming the three of them.

"I'm hungry," Maddie admits.

"I feel like shit, but I bet if my broken arm was fixed, I could eat a horse."

The Reflectives, Gunnar and Slade, turn to Jacky, frowning.

"He means he's normally starved," Maddie explains.

They all continue to stare.

"Jacky wouldn't actually *eat* a horse."

Jacky gives a tight smile. "I don't know—depends. I mean they use them for glue and whatnot."

"How is this relevant?" Merrick asks.

"How indeed?" Slade remarks then turns to Merrick. "If you find a locator, does that mean you'll go straight to Papilio?"

"It's better to have a Sector Ten sphere, of course, but with this many jumps between Beth and me, we can easily locate our home of origin."

Right. "But can you jump Gunnar and me back to One?"

Gunnar puts his hand lightly on Slade's shoulder, shifting Jacky easily to do it. "I have never needed a locator."

Slade frowns. He's not sure he could have managed that comment himself without sounding smug.

"Listen to me, Bloodling," Merrick begins.

"No," Gunnar replies easily. "I am not under Reflective purview. My Kindred Blood is here, and I will be taking her and Slade then returning to One. You and Beth can return to Papilio." Slade raises his black eyebrows. "If you can manage to protect her, otherwise, she might be smart to come with our party. I won't insult her with offering my protection. Though it's painful not to." The ghost of a smile hovers on the Bloodling's lips, and Beth smiles.

Merrick's eyes bulge. "Reflective Jasper is my soul mate and partner. She is not traveling to the lawlessness of Sector One."

Beth turns, placing her hand on Merrick's arm.

Slade seethes at the gesture.

"Jeb."

His eyes soften.

"We need to get Rachett."

His gaze goes hard at the mention of their leader. "Not without Calvin—Kennet."

"Kennet remains on One," she explains. "You know this. With me, you, and Kennet, we should have more than enough Reflectives to reacquire Rachett and restore order."

"Ryan *will* jump. That hopper couldn't keep still and smart if he had a blade against his throat," Slade comments dryly.

"Your directive to not end that hopper utterly lacks of any form of self-preservation." Gunnar's exhale is rough.

"Yeah, all their glamorous directives get in the way of getting shit done." Jacky grimaces. "Let's do something. I'm in a lot of pain, guys."

"He'll heal regardless of where we jump, Jeb." Beth's eyes search his face. "Be reasonable. At this point, order is tenuous in Papilio. It's more critical we grab Rachett then jump home than to jump home without our leader."

"He could be dead," Merrick admits quietly, glancing at Slade for a heartbeat.

"Yes, but I couldn't stand knowing he lived and we didn't try for him."

"I can act as a focus and jump us all." Gunnar meets Merrick's scowl dead-on.

"Jeb, he's my father."

Merrick's face gets that stubborn look that Slade recognizes only too well. "He's Bloodling."

Gunnar's brows drop above his eyes, shadowing an already black gaze. "Are you implying I would jump my blooded daughter into peril? Really, hopper?"

Merrick pegs his hands on his hips. "No, I am not. But I can't foresee every inevitability. And that, as her soul mate, scares the shit out of me."

"Go, Merrick," Jacky says listlessly.

"Please." Beth is trying to reason with an unreasonable Merrick.

Good fortune, Tiny Frog. He's an insufferable male, as all Reflectives are. Full of himself and his own perceived self-importance.

"All right," Merrick says, lightly touching her chin. "For you."

"For me, buttmunch. I'm injured." Jacky shoots a sullen glare Merrick's way.

The corners of Merrick's lips lift. "Maybe you factor into my decision a small amount."

Slade knows Gunnar could have forced the jump. He also knows why he did not.

Slade looks to Beth.

Tiny Frog stares right back, her dark gaze defiant. His feelings swell, tightening his chest, and he realizes Beth is his weakness. And Achilles' heel.

That worries Slade. Immensely.

10

Beth

Beth is very aware of the discord between Jeb and Slade.

For now, she'll ignore it. With her home world's chaos, Jacky's broken wing, and the impending mission to rescue Rachett, she can't worry about the testosterone tug-of-war that's brewing between the males.

She studies Jacky, troubled about how quiet he's become. He should heal during the jump.

Should.

But what if he doesn't? Will he revert to eighteen cycles again? Those are good questions that Beth doesn't have ready answers for.

"Will the locator still be here?" Slade asks, and Jeb slides a glance his way.

"Should be, though we had a rough encounter the last time we were here."

Rough encounter. Beth smiles. Meeting a reanimated human is more than a "rough encounter" in her mind, but she doesn't comment.

Beth surveys the land, seeing the same decaying remnants of turn-of-the-last-century brick architecture that remain in the valley of the Kent Quadrant. Before the farms that grew this world's food for this quadrant were cut short. She spies the exact alley where the zombie ran full tilt in their direction.

Beth briefly wonders what became of him. Raising her eyes, she can just make out the hidden port where the Reflectives' locator is held.

Jeb takes her hand, and she feels the heat of his anticipatory leap tingling between their touch. He glances at her briefly, and Beth gives the barest nod. They jump without a word. The distance is so small that the sting of the leap is only a brief bite before they land at a precariously hung fire escape that suffers from disuse.

Metallic spray paint has haphazardly been overlaid on the original sooty onyx finish.

Jeb tracked the point of reflection and Beth lent him her signature, the same process for any jump, long or short. When they became corporal then solid again, they reappeared almost instantly beside the rotting bars that once held sturdy ladders for escape in case of fire. An archaic practice.

Feels good to jump, Beth thinks before a shrill whistle reaches her ears.

"A little warning, daughter," Gunnar calls from below them.

Beth gives him a stiff hand signal to go back into hiding. His shoulders slump, and he trudges his big form over and repositions behind the dumpster. Bloodlings do not like to skulk in camouflage. It's a proud race and not one for hiding.

The beings of Three do not yet use their garbage as fuel, so there is a perfect spot where the Bloodlings can stay until she and Jeb can sort this mess.

Beth shakes her head. Three is primitive in many ways. However, the Threes are not primitive in the ways of weapons. For all their technology, they pollute their world, though Beth has foreknowledge of when that will stop. And she remembers the directive of The Cause they've already transgressed. *Twelfth: Disturb not the continuum.*

She frowns. There have been many directives she and Jeb have needed to break. Lives were at stake. Sometimes their own.

Jeb runs his hands along the brick, his brows meeting. "Can't remember…there!" he says with a triumphant flash of teeth. A fine crack, seen only if sought, appears beside where the locator sphere would be. Beth had been able to make out the location but not the exact position. The port is meant to be nearly seamless so as to avoid detection by the people of this world.

Beth hands her ceramic dagger to Jeb. "See if you can't pry it open." Without a sister locator, the port does not open automatically.

Jeb glances at her, taking the stout blade by the hilt. "Let us hope I don't inadvertently drop the one sphere we have."

They exchange a look of dread.

Beth looks at the alleyway below them and can just make out her father, Jacky, Slade, and Maddie crouching behind the huge refuse container. They'd discussed making themselves as scarce as possible when they reached the area where the locator was. Their group doesn't need to be out on display. Slade and Gunnar look exactly like what they are here on Three—aliens.

Three is a paranoid world. Paranormal talents were discovered by geneticist Kyle Hart, and subsequently the genetic markers were tampered with by the brilliant but insane Zondorae brothers. Those realities have softened the public consciousness toward all things strange and unusual—but Three is not ready for Bloodling with their giant, almost seven-foot-tall bodies and gray-skinned flesh. With fangs.

No, they reluctantly agreed to stay hidden until they could secure a smooth exit from this world.

Jeb works diligently on the cracked side, inching the blade back and forth, trying to gently pry the port open so they can grab the sphere. Normally, they would have the mate. Two Reflectives would use their own sphere, which in turn would hone in on the stationary one always housed in a port on a jumping sector, and sensing its twin, the port would smoothly open.

Unfortunately, neither of them had their sphere because of Ryan.

Taking the locating sphere from its port is not illegal per se, but it means any Reflective tasked with jumping to this quadrant would need to find another quadrant with a locator. They're deliberately widely spaced.

Jeb finally meets success, but the port opens in jerky movements instead of the smoothness of a normal opening coaxed by its mated sphere. Instead of the small lever that houses the sphere gliding open, it spits apart and sends the sphere rocketing out like an expelled seed pit.

Beth hops to the rail, balances for a split second on the balls of her feet, then leaps.

"Beth!" Jeb bellows.

Beth tracks the sphere midair. Of course, if the cylindrical honing device lands while she uses it to jump, she dies. Even she cannot heal the damage from a five-story fall.

Her body heats, coalescing into weighted molecules of singular purpose as she hits the perfectly prepared medium for Reflectives to jump.

Beth also watches the ground draw closer as her body and the sphere collide.

She immediately seeks reflection. Nothing.

The grains within the asphalt become visible as the ground appears to hurtle toward her.

With bone-jarring pain, she feels something snatch the sphere out of the air, and her along with it, causing her to separate harshly from the reflection.

Beth becomes solid again, groaning.

Slade holds her. It was he who severed her from her reflection.

"You were falling," he says somewhat breathlessly. Not from being out of shape. His eyes are anxious. Slade was worried.

Beth nods, breathing through the agony. It feels as though a part of her body has been amputated. She spares an assessing glance at the ground a meter beneath her and decides the sickening pain is worth the price. "That sometimes happens in a jump."

Gunnar's face appears beside Slade. His expression is ferocious, his lips pulled back from fully extended fangs. "That was *not* funny."

Beth swallows twice before she can speak, plucking the sphere away from Slade. Holding it high in the air, she feels when Jeb uses the surface to appear.

And a nanosecond later, he does.

"If it shattered, we would have lost our easy way to One. Now Gunnar doesn't have to." Beth coughs, and blood coats the inside of her mouth like metallic slime.

She assesses. *Internal bleeding. Cracked ribs. Dislocated shoulder.*

Rough descent. Maybe inertia is good for the moment. Beth looks over at Gunnar from the cradle of Slade's arms. "I did what I must."

"Beth," Jeb says, running a finger over her forehead, "you could have died."

Jeb looks shaken. A rare thing for him.

Beth keeps her eyes on her partner. A male that wants so much more from her. She clenches her jaw. "We're Reflective. It's the nature of our role." Her hand moves to her side.

She's suddenly embarrassed. "Slade, set me down."

He does, and Beth bites her lip. Jacky won't be the only one using the jump to heal.

"I scent your injuries." Slade scowls, his hand hovering beside her elbow.

Gunnar and Jeb scowl as well.

Beth hobbles away from the males.

Jeb's face twists, and she can clearly see what it costs him not to go to her.

She did what she had to do. Beth will heal. But as Jacky would say, she feels like ass.

Maddie approaches and slides an arm around Beth's waist. "I'll help. Lean on me." She gives the men a look of chastisement.

Beth appreciates that, as she doesn't have the energy to spare them the same regard.

"Here, Jeb," Beth says, handing the sphere to him.

He takes it gingerly. Their fingers touch, and a tingle goes through her like an electrical shock, and she groans. The charged sensation feels good—and bad. A sphere between two Reflectives is a powerful conduit of energy.

"'Kay, let's get going," Jacky says. His skin is ashen, and he's trembling.

"Halt!"

They turn. Beth pivots too fast, sucking an inhale from the pain the movement cost her, the shoulder Slade yanked out of the socket throbs like a rotten tooth.

And there at the end of the alley is a Three lawman. *Principle help them*, of all the terrible fortune.

"What is *that*?" Gunnar asks in a hiss.

"Cops," Jacky says then looks at Merrick. "Jump our asses out of here. They get a load of the fang parade and we're toast. They'll interrogate us until I'm legal to drink."

Beth would laugh if she could breathe through it. She spits a wad of phlegm-coated blood. It splatters the asphalt, resembling a gory snail. Beth needs this jump. Badly. She cradles her arm.

Slade and Jeb look at what she expunged, then her.

"How bad?" Jeb asks. His expression is neutral, which tells Beth how worried he is.

"Not good," she replies honestly. "Can't you tell?"

"Police! Hold your position." The voice is closer, and Beth glances at the striding lawman.

Merrick's lips flatten, his eyes on the encroaching Three. "No, not since…" He doesn't finish, and Beth suddenly realizes the soul mate change has altered what was normal between them before.

The lawman draws nearer, his weapon raised.

"Remind me to put in a protocol that this locator be moved."

Beth gives Jeb a weak smile. "Duly noted."

She sags against Maddie and tightens her hold around the taller girl.

"I'll kill him," Gunnar says.

Beth's eyes shut. *Sixth: Take life only in defense of another.* "No," Beth whispers. "Jeb, jump us."

He turns to her. "I need you for One."

Oh no. Beth can't offer her skills; she's too weakened. "Gunnar," Beth says.

"I am here, daughter."

Beth squeezes her eyes shut. "Take my hand."

He does.

"I *will* shoot!"

Beth opens her eyes, sighting in on the lawman. Her vision is ten times that of a Three and more than that of the average Reflective, especially at night, thanks in part to her Bloodling ancestry.

She assesses him instantly. Six feet, Hispanic descent, over forty cycles, moves with precision.

Martial arts training. IQ over one hundred twenty.

Beth knows this male.

"Jeb," her voice resonates.

Jeb's face whips to hers, and she feels his heat, the heat of the jump, a moment before the first bullet takes Beth in the leg.

Gunnar crouches, Jacky in one arm, Beth's hand held in the other. He hisses as Beth's leg blows apart.

Hollow point ammunition. She feels the hole in the back of her leg and knows it's wide as a dinner plate.

She can't help her scream.

"Beth!" Jeb yells.

Then everything fades, the world narrowing to a pinpoint of the lawman centered in her tunneling vision, the edges gray like dirty lace.

The second bullet follows the first, and Jeb moves before it as he jumps them.

Later, Beth knows that he's saved her life.

In that moment of becoming a jumping ribbon of molecules, she knows only that her partner's been hit by a lethal weapon on Three.

She feels the pocket of jumping power lost like a dropped rope and is too weak to focus.

Beth reaches out to Gunnar on the same wavelength that she would seek another Reflective and finds nothing.

Then a tailwind appears, and with her last remaining bit of strength, she holds on to the only one she senses.

Taking Beth from Three—and somewhere else.

11

Merrick

Jeb feels the puncture of a bullet as it passes through his body harmlessly, missing Beth by a hair.

Unfortunately, the avoidance maneuver took a great deal of skill to exist in the corporal realm and not jump simultaneously. Staying in that form without jumping is dangerous, an almost stasis limbo state that, if kept too long, can mean death to a Reflective.

Dangerous but necessary. Jeb wasn't sure that Beth could survive two wounds from the type of ammunition that lawman was using. He can hardly bear the feel of her agony as her leg was torn apart.

The type of bullets, those that enter benignly only to make a huge hole on exit, are extremely difficult to survive. Had Beth been human, she'd already be dead.

The avoidance of that second bullet caused Jeb to have to drop that critical signature. The decision was to let the tether of his jump go or lose Beth.

He let it go.

Only for a moment.

Now Jeb's guts drop in his stomach as he spins toward One—assuming that Gunnar can get them there. He lends his power to the jump, and the line pulls taut, tying everyone together in a hard pull of knotted molecules.

The landing is hard, but Jeb's suffered harder. He falls forward and rolls into the drop. Sand works its way into every crack in his clothing and every pore of his skin. He sits back on his knees, spitting the fine sand out like spoiled sugar.

Giving swift attention to his surroundings, Jeb spots the others immediately and rises to his feet. He dusts off his filthy uniform and finally gives up. There's no cleaning dirt layered upon dirt.

He looks for Beth.

Nothing.

His eyes sweep the others quickly.

Principle no! "Where's Beth?" he yells to Gunnar, who is lifting Maddie by the elbow.

He shakes his head. "I had hold of her hand, and then it was as though the jump went wild."

The jump went wild because Jeb needed to save Beth. But now she isn't here.

Despair soaks Jeb's guts as a pounding headache settles in for the duration.

"Where is she, hopper?" Slade grates, moving toward Jeb with the grace of a native.

The sand doesn't slow the giant Bloodling, for he's accustomed to navigating it.

Jeb sees the blow coming and lets it happen.

He deserves it. He didn't save Beth. He let her jump somewhere without him, gravely injured.

Slade's fist plows into Jeb's unprotected jaw, and he flies backward. But years of training don't depart a Reflective because of despondency.

Jeb's hands snap out, catching himself and rolling to his side as Slade advances.

Slade reaches for Jeb, and Jeb catches the Bloodling's forearm, pulling with all his might, and the big male falls forward.

Jeb kicks Slade square in the ass, and he flies forward as Jeb springs to his feet and rounds toward him.

Now it is the Bloodling's turn to spit sand.

They circle each other.

"You fucking clod," Slade seethes, "you've lost her. Beth cannot be the one you proclaim her to be or you would not have let her go. You lie, hopper."

"I had no choice, Bloodling!" Jeb shouts in his face. If Slade's hair were not still tied down, the force of Jeb's voice would have blown it back.

"Hey guys—the fuck?"

Jeb dare not turn toward Jacky, or Slade will brain him. This, he knows.

Jacky moves from behind him and stands between them.

He is no longer a youngling. Again.

"So Jasper's off"—Jacky makes a seesawing motion with his hand—"gallivanting around somewhere with a bigass hole in her leg, bleeding out, while you guys try to pound each other." Jacky nods, flipping back his longish dark blond bangs. His intense green eyes narrow on the two of them. "Makes perfect sense."

"Sometimes I hate you," Slade says, straightening.

Jacky shrugs. "Whatever. Needed to get you two dicks to cool your jets. Beth's somewhere while you guys are thumping your chests and stuff."

"He's right," Gunnar acknowledges, giving a thorough perusal to Jacky's altered form.

Maddie circles the two of them. "She was already hurt from when Slade caught her. Now Beth's been shot?"

Jeb plugs his hands on his hips. "Yes. The lawman had fired a second shot, and I had to stay corporal for longer than what is deemed safe so the bullet would not strike—"

"—and also not follow our tail," Gunnar finishes.

Jeb gives a grim nod. "It's exactly that." He shoots a rage-filled glance at Slade.

Who glares right back, of course. Though it pleases Jeb that Slade looks positively green from the jump, his skin slicked with sick sweat.

Jeb assesses everyone, ignoring Slade. Maddie and Jacky look whole and well, though Jeb notices Jacky's arm isn't quite right. He walks to the boy.

"Let me look at your arm."

Jacky lifts it. There's a scar where the break occurred. "A healer would be good."

Jacky pointedly looks around them. "Yup. Ton of 'em milling around, I notice."

Jeb scowls. "Who will jump with me again?"

Gunnar looks at Maddie. "I love my daughter, but there is nothing that can take me from my Kindred Blood."

"I'm sticking with Mad. You can go off and white knight it, Merrick. You're great at that."

Jeb's frustration is at an all-time high.

"Truce, Merrick." Slade interrupts Jeb's glower and reaches out his hand but not before he licks his parched lips.

Beth needs me. And...I need Slade.

Merrick will seek help from whatever source if it sees Beth safe.

Slade is a traitor and a competitor for Beth's affection. Merrick knows this. But deep down, he's certain the Bloodling cares for her. Even if he is not aware of this himself.

Jeb wraps his fingers around the bigger male's hand, and they give one sharp, bone-crunching shake.

He turns to Jacky. "I need something from you."

At every turn, Jacky is an immature, goading youngling. But his reply nearly brings Jeb to tears. No small feat.

"Anything, bud."

"Tell Reflective Kennet what has occurred, what I will do. And that upon my return, we'll attempt a rescue of Commander Rachett."

Jacky whistles low and long, scraping a palm back and forth across his head. "We sorta put Kennet out of his misery so he wouldn't follow Jasper."

Jeb struggles to remain calm, lifting a filthy hand to wipe sweat from his brow. "Did you kill him?"

They stare at each other for a weighted moment.

"Hell no, Merrick. He's one of the good guys."

Jeb grins suddenly. "Yes he is. Tell him not to kill you, okay?" Jeb says in Three.

Jacky smiles. "Believe me, it'll be the first thing I do."

Maddie comes forward and hugs Jeb.

He gives her an awkward hug back. "Find her. She's the only girlfriend I have."

Jeb looks down at her, his brows meeting. "Girlfriend?"

She smiles, nodding. "Yeah, Merrick, if Beth had an even vaguely normal existence, she'd have other girls to hang with." One side of her lips lifts, and she laughs.

Jeb frowns harder then releases her.

Slade comes to stand by Merrick's side. "I loathe you, hopper."

Jeb nods. "And I, you."

"But we shall find Beth together."

Jeb turns his head, meeting that black bloodshot gaze dead-on. "Yes we will."

They move to the lake, leaving the others behind, though they watch their progress.

"How will we jump?"

Jeb chuckles. "She is my soul mate. I will find her."

Slade's expression is tense. "I'm troubled, Merrick. She was gravely injured."

"Yes."

"*Where* has she landed?"

Neither one articulates that if she's repositioned herself somewhere on Three, she'll be easy pickings for Ryan to stumble across.

And there is no doubt in either of their minds that he will eventually pursue them.

"I should have killed him."

Slade's face whips to Jeb. "What about your precious directive?"

Jeb says nothing for a time. Then he admits what he really feels. "Fuck that, I think."

Slade laughs abruptly, his short fangs peeking out from between his lips. "I like that change of heart, Reflective."

Jeb sighs, already feeling the heat of the jump building inside his body. "For her, it seems there's no rules."

Slade doesn't reply. Which is almost its own answer.

⁓

Something's stabbing Beth's back.

She lifts a hand without opening her eyes and feels for what it might be.

Grass.

Beth lifts her heavy eyelids. Long stalks of faded green, feathery-looking pasture grass grow all around her, swaying gently in a mild breeze of what appears to be late summer.

Placing both palms at her sides, she hikes herself into a sitting position.

Blood has soaked through her clothes. She places her hand on the wound and finds it's still leaking. Beth tries to steady her breathing, but she's scared.

She cannot feel her legs.

That can mean only one thing. A fragment of the ammunition has nicked something critical. Something beyond her body's capacity to heal. Tears shimmer, skating across her vision and promising to fall.

The pain is enough to keep them at bay if she concentrates on the horrible sensations.

Beth decides to swallow her grief. Feeling sorry for herself and giving in to the compulsion to burst into tears will not help her.

Self-pity never does.

The powers of Reflective healing have corrected the terrible reactive jump she made before when Slade captured her in his arms, arresting her from being a warm, shattered splat on Three asphalt. She tests her arm, swinging it wide. The limb moves smoothly.

It does not appear as though this other grievous wound will correct itself.

Jeb will come.

But perhaps not soon enough. Because Beth has just now easily determined where she landed, and for the life of her, she can't understand why.

The large, opaque spheres, half buried in the soft earth, are her first clue.

The Band and the criminal Zondorae leavings of Fragment roam this sector. And here she lies, crippled from the waist down.

Marvelous.

Beth inspects her wound quite thoroughly. Which is no trouble, considering she has no feeling in the area. The bleeding has stopped, but the exit wound is a huge hole in her leg. There is no talking herself out of the mess. She will always be scarred—if she survives.

She's very happy to note her ceramic blade is intact and at hand.

Based on the sun's position, Beth gauges the time of day to be nearly five o'clock. Her stomach chooses that moment to give an appreciative roar. When was the last time they ate?

She looks around her. No one is here but she. The overwhelming loneliness of her situation strikes her like a deadly weapon.

I will concentrate on the basest needs. Water—food. Nothing else. Beth can mourn and gnash her teeth later.

So she sits in the ocean of wheat and waits for the sun to sink. Minutes take hours, and she licks her lips. Terrible thirst assails her, and each swallow is a parched slide without saliva.

Bloodred light begins to creep across the pasture, tinting the tall stalks of wheat to flags of crimson. The entire grassland appears as if it's ablaze.

Beth is mournful, thirsty, hungry, paralyzed, and fearful. But she admires the beauty of that crystalline moment of the day ceding to night, thanking Principle she still lives to see nature's spectacle.

The huge single ball of sector Thirteen's sun sinks like a scarlet stone, and Beth sighs with its absence. Heat flees as dark sets in like teeth in black velvet.

She lies down and rolls over onto her elbows, preparing to crawl to the border of forest where surely there is water.

Beth comes face-to-face with beings she's not seen before.

Her heartbeats pile on top of each other as her vague unsettled feeling turns into outright terror.

Or has she seen them before?

12

Merrick

"Must you touch me?"

Jeb tips his eyes skyward at the same time he grabs the back of Slade's grimy tunic, fisting the tough leather material just enough to maintain contact.

"Yes," Jeb answers in a clipped voice.

Slade crosses his arms. "I can't abide jumping."

Jeb's lips quirk. "Yet you must."

Slade straightens his shoulders and nods. "For Tiny Frog."

Jeb scowls, gripping Slade's tunic tighter.

The heat of the jump washes over him, the cold lake water lapping at the toes of his boots—reflecting—as does the entire lake. The two suns, weak by Papilio or Three standards, are low in the sky, and Slade winces from the exposure.

The soft sunlight of this world is perfect for Bloodlings. True vampires could not survive any degree of daylight. But as Jeb understands it all, vampire is only one part of the Bloodling ancestry. The other? That is yet undetermined. If ever there is a time in the future when Papilio is righted back to its noble Cause, perhaps visiting the unexplored sectors is a good place to begin.

Flames of ice and heat drive up from Jeb's feet, bursting at his core and shooting sparks of popping current to his fingertips. The fine hairs on his head lift slightly, and he zeroes in on a break of waves coming toward them.

Sunlight bleeds across the peaks as the late afternoon sun dies against the water.

Jeb tracks.

A moment later, a tense Slade and he slam into the tip of one sparkling chunk of water and are through.

Once in a jump, Jeb immediately senses Beth's tail and hurtles them through the molecular dust of her leap.

As he readies for landing, simultaneous thoughts crowd his brain.

Why this sector—*and what other tail is he sensing?*

Jeb releases Slade so he doesn't drag him, and when the big Bloodling lands, it's palms first, in a slide very much like the game the Threes play. Basebat? Basketbat? Jeb doesn't remember.

Slade rolls over, spitting grass and dirt from his mouth and gifting Jeb with a foul expression.

Jeb's mood immediately improves.

"It will never get better. You don't have a bit of Reflective in your veins."

Slade groans, rolling over and sitting on his ass, breathing deeply.

The Bloodling does look very bad, positively green.

"Throw up and get it over with."

Slade scowls.

Stubborn male.

They stare at each other, and when it appears Slade is working through the agony of the jump, Jeb turns his attention elsewhere.

He surveys their surroundings. Mercifully, night has fallen, and though Jeb has a lot of hate for the Bloodling, as Jacky would phrase it, he needs him. And if the Bloodling doesn't get over this jumping sickness, he's of no use to Jeb. Nighttime will be easier for Slade.

Because right now, they've landed in Sector Thirteen. Dangerous and primitive in the extreme, the criminal remnant from Three has been unceremoniously tossed onto this world and perfectly named as Fragment.

The Band, and the people housed inside the decaying biospheres are somewhat protected from this middle criminal element who roam between the great forests of pine where the Band reside and the biospheres that hold the remnants of humans who once lived Outside.

However, Jeb knows the protection of the spheres is coming to an end. Before this debacle of dissent happened when Rachett was overthrown, it had come before the council of Reflectives that Sector Thirteen would need assistance in its transition to the Outside. Or the people who lived within the spheres would be decimated by the ones who maundered outside of it.

The Fragment would need to be subdued, or permanently contained, in a prison of the Reflectives' making.

For now, Papilio needed to be put back to order, then Reflectives could get back to soldiering.

Well, no longer for Jeb. His timepiece had ceased. Technically, that meant that he was no longer under the dictates of The Cause.

As though sensing Jeb's thoughts, Slade finally speaks. "Why are you still policing? Beth has explained that your commitment to The Cause is no more once you find your"—he pauses over his next words, making the break in his sentence awkward—"soul mate."

"I was just considering that. Here I am, trying to locate Beth while concerns of this world suffocate me."

Slade smirks. "Looks as though you can take the male out of the Reflective but not the Reflective out of the male."

Jeb doesn't comment, nonplussed at the other male's insights.

"Where are we, Reflective Merrick?" Slade asks after a protracted silence. He stands, brushing off his clothes.

"Sector Thirteen."

Slade's black eyebrows rise.

Jeb's exhale is exhausted. He has been more tired, more thin on patience during his lifetime.

But not by a good measure.

"Is this a good world?" Slade tilts his head, giving Jeb critical study, and after a moment, he adds, "Your silence tells me no."

Jeb's exhale is long. "You would be correct."

"Tell me."

Jeb does.

Slade shifts his weight, folding his arms. "So these derelict humanoids maunder between these globe houses—" He sweeps his palm toward the spheres.

"—spheres."

Slade inclines his head. "Yes, yes. *Spheres*." Slade looks out over the windswept pastureland. And though both males are impervious to anything but true cold, the wind bites—the promise of autumn near. "And they take the women and breed them, kill whatever males who roam. What of this Band?"

"They are the result of a genetic tampering. When there wasn't enough clean air to breathe after the natural disaster of the asteroid's impact, they evolved with breathing slits." Jeb indicates both sides of his own throat.

Slade snorts. "It doesn't sound plausible."

"Uh-huh. And nightlopers and Bloodlings are perfectly normal in comparison."

"Yes," Slade replies abruptly.

Both males burst out laughing, and Jeb realizes how terribly exhausted they both are to laugh at such things.

"Where is Beth?" Slade suddenly asks.

Jeb can vaguely scent her. But for reasons unknown, her tailwind ends abruptly here.

"Do you sense her?" Slade asks sharply, his eyes narrowing. The black orbs of his gaze reflect like oil in the nearly moonless night. Only the thinnest crescent winks in and out from behind skittish clouds.

Jeb feels the back of his neck heat. "Not very well," he finally admits.

"Well, what good are you, hopper?" Slade squeezes out from between his lips. "We're half-starved, in the middle of an inhospitable world, with Tiny Frog out here somewhere injured."

Shame slicks Jeb's insides. "I *understand* all that. Do you have any suggestions, you arrogant Bloodling prince? Because I have duly briefed you. I don't want the Fragment or Band to have advantages over us because you do not comprehend the inherent danger of this place."

Slade meets him, their chest butting. "I understand danger, Reflective Merrick. And grief. And sacrifice. Just because you are Reflective does not mean you are the only noble creature in this vast universe."

They step away from each other, their chests heaving.

"The priority is Beth," Jeb says, enunciating each word like a punch.

"Agreed."

Jeb grits his teeth. "You have the better nose between us. *You* track her."

"I will track her, Merrick. Just as soon as I can separate the other scents."

Jeb's jaw slides back and forth, and he grips his hips with his hands, leaning forward. "*What* other scents?"

Slade dips his head, his nostrils flaring wide. "Lowly. Primate—*other*. I have not scented this particular fragrance before. But I am afraid."

Jeb jerks his chin up. "You—afraid?"

Slade nods slowly. "There is a legend, spoken about from my people for eons, about a race that began us all."

Jeb shakes his head. He doesn't believe this line of conversation. "Oh? And who would these ancient beings be?"

"They inhabit all the worlds."

Jeb crosses his arms.

"They are called First Species by my people, and others, if rumor and legend hold true."

"And what makes them a threat?" Jeb is uneasy, for why would Slade unveil an untruth when Beth's whereabouts are at stake? And why had he not heard of this race?

"They hold a piece of all of us within the fabric of their being."

Jeb stills like a statue, thinking his words through. If what Slade said were true, they would be a very challenging enemy.

Jeb's eyes latch onto the Bloodling.

"Do they have Beth?"

Slade lifts his shoulders. "I am not sure, but assuming they do is better."

Jeb snorts. "Better for whom?"

Slade looks toward the woods. "Better for Tiny Frog."

"Well, who do we have here?" the giant male asks.

Beth searches him and those who came with him. She can't survive this. And that is fine.

A calmness steals over her. She will not be fodder for rapists or brutes or be tortured for knowledge about Papilio.

Beth will get close to this leader then end her own life.

He somehow reminds her of Slade in a vague way. He is nearly two and a half meters tall, and a fine downy layer of dark brown hair covers his body, with an extreme brow ridge hunching over extraordinarily beautiful slowly revolving amber eyes.

Looking at that gaze dead-on does something to Beth. Calms her.

A chirping sound garners the leader's attention. "She is injured, Alpha."

The leader turns his attention to her, his brows going low. "I am Ulric."

Beth blinks. "I am Reflective Jasper."

He frowns, his massive arms bunching as he folds them. "A traveler?"

Beth is familiar with the misuse of the term. She covertly palms her blade in her hand and slides it along her thigh.

"No—I am a natural-born jumper. A soldier from Sector Ten."

"You? A soldier." The corners of his lips pull up, and the males look at one another.

Oh, for the use of my legs. Alas, Beth doesn't have that. She must make do with what she does have—her wits.

And reflection.

A belt of some kind hangs from Ulric's tapered hips. The males wear short tunics that just cover what makes them male, but not much is left to the imagination.

Beth's face heats as Ulric's nostrils flare.

"You desire us?" he asks in a soft voice.

Absolutely not, Beth thinks. "You are not very well covered up. I'm...uncomfortable."

Ulric smiles. "Modesty. A comely trait." He lifts his chin. "We'll take you to our clan, heal you."

"No," Beth says in a low voice, and Ulric halts from the step he took nearer to her.

Beth sights the hanging blade from his weapons belt. *Obsidian.*

Perfect.

The Reflection tears through her, undoing some of the partial healing she accomplished to jump so soon after landing.

She hits Ulric soundly, staggering him, and grabs onto his tightly cinched belt with her left hand and lifts the dagger with her right.

Their gaze locks.

"You cannot hurt me, little female."

She nods, her lower body sagging uselessly behind her. "That is not my intent."

Beth cuts her own throat.

She thinks of Jeb and Slade, hoping they'll be safe without her in this world.

Ulric's whiskey-colored eyes widen, his hands seizing her by the shoulders.

But Beth is already choking on her own blood.

13

Slade

"We can*not* charge in there and expose ourselves."

Merrick gives Slade a disgusted look, clearly aching to hit him.

"Listen to me. I know you'd rather go headlong into battle."

Merrick's lips thin. "The sooner we get Beth—"

"We hurt Beth's chances if we die trying to rescue her without stealth. You *know* this, Merrick—think."

Merrick's exhale is raw, and he stalks away. Slade allows him time to fume.

After a full minute of silence, Merrick slowly walks back to Slade, his heavy boots kicking a path through the long grass stalks.

"All right, Bloodling—what do you propose?"

Slade's certain his expression is grim. "If it *is* a First Species clan, and they are as ancient as I've been told, then they will respect ancient ways. Females are scarce in this sector?"

Merrick gives a terse nod, a slight furrow forming between his eyes.

"So Beth would be valuable just because of her gender." Slade grasps his chin. "I propose that I stake a claim. If I do that, I can fight—duel, whatever they refer to it as—win my right to have her as my female."

Merrick's fair skin suffuses with red, and his mouth hangs slightly agape. "Is *this* your machination? To claim Beth under the guise of this current catastrophe?"

Slade snorts. "If I could only have been so clever, hopper. Let me see"—he taps his chin—"I first make sure Beth is shot with a type of Three exploding ammunition, then I let her sail off to the wrong sector, where she is summarily scooped up by a dangerous species who inhabit a sector where the males outnumber the females…" Slade raises his eyebrows.

"Fifteen to one," Merrick supplies in clipped tones.

Slade tips his head back. "Ah—yes. Could I but sort all those occurrences with that exacting precision."

"Shut up." Merrick glares.

Slade smirks.

After another precious minute slides by, Merrick replies, "Fine."

Slade nods. "In the event that we don't have any misunderstandings, I will claim Beth for the express purpose of her rescue."

They stare at each other.

Merrick grits his teeth and gives another terse nod.

"I'll follow my nose." Slade taps the bridge of his nose and winks at Merrick.

"What if they kill you?"

Slade walks to where Merrick stands. "They may or may not have hopper genetics. But we can't be sure, eh?"

Merrick looks down, scrubbing a palm over his face. "No."

"Then get something that reflects—anything. And if whatever I attempt doesn't work, get her the hades out of here."

Merrick's chin lifts, his eyes blazing. "Really?"

Slade twists his lips. "Yes. She is more than we know, Merrick. More important than you and me and our paltry existence. Beth Jasper is pure of heart."

Suddenly Slade whips his head toward the woods, his nostrils flaring.

"What?" Merrick asks sharply.

"It's Beth." Slade hears the panic in his own voice.

Merrick grips his shoulder.

"Her blood, hopper—I smell her blood."

All color drains from Merrick's face. "Have they—?"

Slade shakes his head, yanking himself out of the Reflective's grip and striding toward the woods. Toward the scent of Beth's essence draining.

"I do not know. But I know this—it's more blood than she can live without."

Merrick catches up, and Slade whirls. "Stay here. Let me do what I can. What we discussed."

The hopper hisses better than a Bloodling. "This is killing me."

Slade shakes his head and jogs to the forest's edge.

When he reaches the border of wheaten pastureland bleeding into the dense trees, he stops.

The site of Beth, ashen and with a cut throat, robs his breath.

His hope.

Slade forgets the things he told Merrick.

He charges in to save Beth.

Fuck this, Jeb thinks before racing after Slade.

If Beth is gravely hurt enough for the Bloodling to smell her blood—and the quantum? Whether Jeb lives or dies is of no consequence.

Slade sprints into the woods, and a symphony of whistles and chirping sounds race after him. Jeb follows.

It is night. The birds have roosted. He slaps branches aside and peers through the dim woods.

Jeb frowns, sighting a flash of metal with something's movement, and doesn't allow himself to think. He tracks, reflecting at the momentary illumination.

One second he is standing in the vast blond field at the forest's border, and the next instant he finds himself among a group of huge males of primate origin but somehow similar to the Bloodling they hold down.

Jeb has to admire Slade. It takes six of the males to contain him.

Their eyes lock for a suspended brutal moment of understanding as Slade gives silent communication to Jeb. Telepathic? *No.* But the look from the male is indisputable.

They come for Jeb with a grace born of the time spent in these deep and mature woods. Long arms and heavily muscled legs bunch and lengthen as they move toward him, and slowly spinning eyes in various shades sight him easily, the blanketing night not slowing their approach.

Jeb's frantic eyes dance among the objects within easy reach, latching onto the thing that got him here.

All the primate males wear weapons belts and tunics.

His gaze trips over a dying Beth, and his guts cinch into a knot. Then he sees something swing freely from one of the males' belts—a blade.

The waning moonlight pierces the forest intermittently, and a vagrant strand strikes the metal of one highly polished dagger.

His eyes meet those of the owner. The color of low sunlight flashes within his gaze. Raw, burning intelligence meets his stare, and Jeb tracks the weapon a split second later.

The male's hand begins to sweep over the metal, but Jeb has already jumped.

And Jeb lands at the feet of the male—flat on his back. Sloppy jumping, but the best he could do in the near dark with poor reflection.

Jeb rolls to his side and grabs onto Beth's ankle. Sliding his hand upward, he wraps her flesh and finds it cool to the touch.

His assessment begins immediately. Ends. Beth's lost too much blood to live—Jeb's thrown backward by a hard blow and inadvertently jerks Beth with him.

"No!" he roars at whoever struck him. "Let me save her, fool!"

The leader, who nearly broke his jaw, jerks him up by his dirty clothing, tearing the neckline away from the shoulder seaming as he does.

He shakes him hard enough to rattle teeth.

Jeb straightens his arm, flat palming the male's broad nose. Blood sprays.

Jeb torques his body, slamming his skull into the male's forehead.

Pain explodes in his own, and Jeb has a moment to realize the male's skull is built like a brick wall.

They fall, and Jeb—woozy, starved, and nearly crazed with fear for Beth—begins to crawl over to where she lies.

"Beth!" Jeb yells, and then he sees it—the wound to end them all.

Jeb sinks to his knees. Wanting to weep, sucking it back in a sick gulp of grief.

The delicate column of her neck is sliced almost through. She's lost so much blood that her skin is whiter than fresh snow, the veins showing through like finely constructed blue lace.

Jeb feels the presence of the First Species behind them.

"Do not hurt the female," the one whose nose he smashed growls from behind Jeb.

Jeb cranes his head and looks behind him. The male's nose is a bloody ruin. "I have no intention of harming her. She is my soul mate."

"She dies," he hisses, throwing his palm toward her. "Obviously, she does not wish for whatever you offer."

Jeb turns his attention back to Beth.

Her eyes are open, and she tries to move, reach out to him. "No—don't, Beth."

"She did it to herself, traveler. I offered to heal her other injuries, and she jumped to me—by my own dagger's reflection—and used her own blade to commit this…horrible act."

Jeb understands why, and it shreds his soul. He shuts his eyes, gripping her chilled hand. Then he remembers the male's words.

Jeb can't heal this; a jump can't heal this.

He faces the male, never letting go of Beth's hand. "What do you mean, heal her?"

The male's eyes slowly revolve in a disconcerting way. Jeb shakes his head, trying to rid himself of the strange sensation of gazing into those hypnotic orbs.

"We can heal most females. But we must act quickly."

"How?" Jeb asks, though he's already passively accepted the fact that whatever they offer—if her life can be spared—it will be worth the outcome.

The leader's dominant brow ridge folds with his expression. "Blood," he says, as though it should be obvious. "I offer blood to save her."

"No!" Slade roars, fighting to swim from underneath the pile of males holding him down.

"Why?" Jeb yells, spinning to face the Bloodling. "If it would spare her life?"

A heartbeat of time thumps past. And the lightest touch lands on Jeb, as though a feather fell on his hand.

It's not. It's Beth's icy touch.

Her eyes are wide, frantic. She doesn't want what the male offers. Jeb can see it within her expression.

However, Beth's will to die is not stronger than Jeb's will to see her live.

Jeb stands, turning swiftly to face the leader. Hostile eyes crawl over him from every corner. "What does this entail?"

"Simple, traveler."

Nothing is simple in Jeb's experience, especially when someone does a favor.

He looks back at Beth and feels her life ebbing.

"Don't, Merrick." Slade cuts Merrick with his eyes.

Jeb stands straighter and ignores Slade. "What must be done?"

The leader turns to the tight group of males. "Let the fanged one go. We will save this female."

He turns back to Jeb. "My name is Ulric, and I am the leader of our clan."

"I am Reflective Jeb Merrick."

Ulric inclines his head then tilts it at the group of other males. "Cyrn."

The largest male rises off one of Slade's limbs and strides silently to Ulric.

"Give the female blood."

Cyrn's lip rises, baring his teeth, and Jeb almost asks why he looks so grim if females are so scarce, but then he replies, "As you wish, Ulric."

He moves to Beth, and Jeb has to physically restrain himself from tearing into the male.

The logic is that if they'd wanted to kill Beth, they could have done so a thousand times before he and Slade arrived.

The male is a quarter meter taller than Jeb. Cyrn narrows his golden eyes on him with obvious disdain before walking past.

Jeb doesn't care about his regard, as long as Beth lives.

Kneeling beside Beth, Cyrn gently slides his hand underneath her slaughtered neck. Lifting his forearm to his mouth, he sweeps his lips across his own flesh.

A gash opens, and deep scarlet blood wells like black oil.

"Drink, female," he instructs.

Beth's eyes are closed, her breathing labored.

"Stubborn woman," he mutters.

Jeb clenches his teeth. "Beth is not stubborn, she's *dying*."

Cyrn's lips twist in obvious irritation. "She has no will to live, traveler. Only a will to leave this place." His exhale is disgusted.

Cyrn sets her head down and pinches his wound tightly, churning more blood from the cut he made with his fangs.

Hovering his arm above her mouth, blood drops fall like jet-black gems.

Beth attempts to twist her face away.

With another impatient exhale, he grips her cheeks, mashing them together, and by default, her lips pucker open.

"Do not hurt her," Jeb warns in a voice barely better than a growl.

"Loathsome traveler, I am not like your kind. We do not harm helpless females. Our females do not self-mutilate to escape their males," Cyrn tosses over his shoulder, his lips flattening into an angry slash.

Jeb's face heats. He doubts very much that was Beth's intent. However, her actions make it possible for others to interpret them another way.

Cyrn massages the portion of her throat that's not cut, gently closing the wound as he does.

Beth sucks whistling breaths through her nose, her eyes panicked. Her arms fly up, trying to grab onto anything.

"She's drowning." Jeb moves forward, and two males grab his arms.

"It is the process, traveler."

"Reflective," Jeb corrects and feels wet heat at the back of his eyelids at Beth's struggle to live.

Finally, Beth swallows.

Then again.

On the third swallow, she lifts a weak hand and wraps Cyrn's wrist, latching her mouth around what he offers. He easily draws her tight against his body.

"That's it, female. You are an ungrateful wretch, but take of my body—my essence—and be well."

Jeb frowns as the male gives his blood with a sort of grim determination, though his words speak to how much he would rather not.

Beth's eyelids flutter shut, and her head tips back. Healthy color begins to bloom on her ashen cheeks.

Cyrn covers her wounded throat with his hand and hauls her against his body more tightly as he continues to feed her, though Beth looks as though she's eating while sleeping.

"Now you've done it, Merrick."

Jeb's head whips to Slade's voice.

"Release me. It's over now."

The males let Jeb go.

Slade's flat eyes meet his.

"It's better she would have died, hopper."

Jeb's eyes narrow on Slade. He could *never* believe that. "Why?"

"Because now she is bound to him." Slade jerks his head toward the large male still feeding Beth.

As Slade tried to bind her?

The bottom drops out of Jeb's stomach, and he turns slowly to Ulric. "Is this true?"

"We have healed the female. I never said the gesture would be without consequence."

Jeb instantly attacks him.

When they beat him into unconsciousness, it's almost a relief.

Thinking about what he let happen to Beth is the alternative. And not one he can stand.

14

Beth

Angry eyes languidly revolve inside a strong face.

He is not handsome, but Beth finds the features he possesses interesting. Taken separately, they aren't special.

Together, they arrest her.

Which, in turn, makes her wary and suspicious.

High cheekbones abut eyes that are deeply set and wickedly sunlit, though Beth senses it's night in the sector of spheres.

Shivering, she hikes the scratchy blanket up to her neck and winces.

That's right, I committed suicide.

Beth shelves what she's done for later recollection. Right now, she's in a confined room with a large male of an alien species.

She continues to study his form. A large brow ridge shadows his warm eyes. A strong Roman nose anchors a face with lips almost too full to belong to a male. His square jaw saves him from appearing too feminine. In addition, a light coating of dark hair covers his body.

"You stare, female?" His derisive tone shocks Beth from her observation.

"Yes," she answers, hiking her chin, prickling at his tone. "You *are* the only being in the room. There isn't much to look at."

"How true," he says, as though being in the same four-meter space as her is a horrible circumstance.

Vague memories crowd her mind. Things he said to her as he fed her blood.

Beth's face flames, and she touches her stomach. *Slade had fed me.* "Thank you," she says with obligatory stiffness.

His face turns to her in profile, and the barest bit of moonlight hits the part she can see perfectly, causing his expression to appear cut in half.

"Do not thank me"—he gives a disdainful chuckle—"thank Ulric." His disconcerting stare meets her eyes. "He *commanded* me to feed you—heal you."

Beth frowns. "I did what I must."

Sector Thirteen is barbaric. Beth made a severe choice based on what she knew. Beth did not know this species roamed Sector Thirteen. That they were capable of showing mercy.

He whirls, hissing, and Beth doesn't flinch. Neither his size nor his nearness intimidates her. She is unafraid of death.

"You do not know what you are, life bearer. That you could take your own life and rob—" He turns his back to her, clearly disgusted with his perception of her actions, his long-fingered hands fisting. "No matter. It is worthless to discuss subjects of value with the valueless."

Beth's offended despite herself. "You do not know me. I couldn't heal what had happened to me. *And*—I thanked you. Don't worry. You won't have to deal with me for much longer."

He turns to face her once more, narrowing his eyes at her. "You go nowhere. You have healing to do."

Beth lifts a shoulder. "I understand what still needs to mend. Another jump in less than a day will right the remainder."

The corner of his full lips turns up. "You were paralyzed from a weapon used against you as well as the wound you carelessly gave yourself."

Beth tosses off the covers and stands. Every bit of her aches, but she can feel. She wiggles her toes.

This creature gave her that. Beth should be grateful. She is.

She's also mad as a hornet.

Beth strides to him, hiding the wince of pain.

He watches her come, unmoving.

She pokes him in the chest, and his eyes widen. "Listen, whatever your name may be, I was deliberate in wounding myself and not a bit"—she jabs her finger against his chest again, and he captures it—"careless," she ends on a hiss.

They stare at each other. "I might hate you, traveler, but I am not immune to your femaleness."

Beth blinks. Hates me?

Femaleness?

He abruptly releases her hand, dropping it as though her touch burns him.

"You don't know anything about me," Beth seethes.

His lips twist, his eyes darkening to deep gold, and he lifts his chin. "I know enough. As soon as Ulric says you are sufficiently healed to travel to wherever you came from, I will be happy to assist your departure."

She crosses her arms, and they glare at each other. "Where are my friends?"

He folds his arms, mirroring her, and Beth can't help but notice the breadth of his chest, the corded muscles of his legs and arms. She's accustomed to large men, warriors. All Reflective males are much larger than the typical men of other sectors. But this male's sheer size should intimidate, especially considering how weak she finds herself.

Beth won't let his attempt to bully her succeed.

"They are not dead—yet," he comments in a dry voice.

What an idiot. Beth decides right then that she doesn't care that he healed her.

But she swallows her pride. "May I see them?"

"Are they both your lovers?" His smirk is smug.

Beth slaps him. Hard. And judging by the backward stagger, he was not anticipating what she could mete.

She has a moment's fierce satisfaction before he grips her and shakes her once, so hard her teeth click together.

Beth gasps as pain like a barbed whip strikes through her body, and her head tilts back. Searing agony tears through her insides, and she moans.

He captures the back of her skull. "Do not strike me again, female." His eyes are molten gold, blazing into her brain.

She attempts to assess him but gets nothing. Beth changes tactics. "Why can't a female travel with males and not have a sexual tie?"

He licks his lips. Doesn't answer. It's the first moment she may have caught him slightly nervous. "Not possible, female."

"My name is Beth."

He releases her, and Beth falls on her rear end, unable to catch herself. She yelps, and he clenches his hands, regret flashing across his expression then leaving as quickly as it appeared.

As Jacky would say, *fuck him twice.*

Beth flat palms the floor and pushes herself up—tears well from the pain. She ignores it. Her hand whips out and hits the rough wood wall, and she uses the surface to slowly walk herself back to the narrow bed she was lying on. Her breaths are measured, deliberate. Every bit of her hurts from taking on the male. From healing more than she can and still not being whole.

Without turning around, Beth stretches out, her back facing the male. Let him kill her or beat her to a pulp. At this point, she doesn't care which.

A scalding tear slips out from beneath her clenched eyes. For an excruciating moment, Beth longs for her death, to end the unbearable pain and uncertainty.

Papilio is in ruins, Jeb and Slade are Principle knows where, and she's got an insane male from an undetermined species and who loathes her existence laughing at her every misfortune.

Yes. As the Threes would say, where is the silver lining in this mess?

Ah. That's right. Ryan hasn't caught up with her yet! But there's time. Oh Principle yes, plenty of time for that. And here she lies, ready and waiting for him to see her death through. Why couldn't she finish him? Is The Cause the only thing that matters? *Really?*

His voice breaks into her thoughts. "I smell your tears."

Something else for him to laugh at. Beth squeezes her lids more tightly and doesn't reply.

The quiet lasts so long that Beth's sure that he's left. She begins to drift, her body's forced healing causing her drowsiness.

"My name is Cyrn."

Beth's eyelids slam open, her heart hammering. She rolls over, seeking him. But he's gone.

As though he never was.

Cyrn

Cyrn swings from the tethered vegetation ropes that the few females of their clan make for silent transport through the tall canopies of forest.

The cogs of his mind lumber through what transpired with the female.

Beth.

A pang of guilt pierces him so strongly he almost misses the next platform. He corrects his sloppiness and swings upward, landing smoothly on his leader's railed porch.

Cyrn is a hundred feet above the ground and glances at the forest floor indifferently. He has been using tethers since infancy. First with his mother and then as a young male who hunted.

Now their species dwindles while the Fragment swells.

Gingerly he touches his cheek where the female—*Beth*—hit him with her tiny hand. He chuckles low in his throat. She struck true.

Why she is an adept fighter is puzzling to Cyrn.

More disturbing is how easily Beth would toss away her own life. What terrible burden must she carry that would decide her fate by her own hand? Cyrn posted guards at his platform, in the happenstance she would try again.

Cyrn looks to the ground. It would be a killing fall from this distance were she to pitch herself over the rail.

After a few moments of morose contemplation, he shakes his thoughts away like cobwebs. The female Beth will leave this place. With her males.

Rage burns like wildfire inside Cyrn. He scented the lust from the other males. Why she denies their connection, he cannot answer. Cyrn shrugs at his own musings. Obviously, any female who would kill herself doesn't know her own mind. A type of lunacy.

"Cyrn?"

He spins, crouching low, his arms swinging in arcs at his side.

Ulric grins, his teeth very bright in the soft nighttime that's moving toward dawn. "It's not easy to surprise you, my friend."

Cyrn straightens, a spontaneous smile spreading on his face. Cyrn adheres to strict hierarchy when others are present, but in private, he and Ulric have been close comrades since birth.

"How fares the female?" he asks softly.

Cyrn shakes his head. "Why, Ulric?"

Ulric casts a circumspect look at Cyrn. "You are unmated."

Cyrn slowly nods, remembering. "I was not lucky enough to be part of the communal mating that occurred a few moons past."

Not long ago, dissenters within neighboring clans tried to break away, and after a battle, lust descended. Not an untypical outcome but one that Cyrn had inadvertently been omitted from as he was guarding the clan.

Now many of his clanmates were mated to women who had been the spoils of that war. Though they were all willing.

First Species have no need of raping or coercing females. They bear life and must be protected at all costs.

Even Beth, as pathetic as she is.

"They are not travelers, you know," Ulric says, tilting his face to Cyrn.

Cyrn perches on a low stool made of wood and bisected tethers from the organic material of the forest.

He leans back, lacing his fingers and resting his spine against one of the tree house poles. The little chair creaks under his weight.

Ulric's domain is the highest platform in the clan, with a thatched roof of mud and the strong, dried stalks of the fields. Roughly octagon, it circles a large evergreen tree, spanning to a twin beside it. The two great trees reek of the freshness of the forest and the bodies within.

Cyrn closes his eyes, inhaling deeply. He's always appreciated natural smells. Loving the forest where their clan dwells is a deep-seated joy inside his heart.

Nothing spoils that. *Until this dimwit female arrived.*

He feels his expression sour, and Cyrn pops forward, dangling his hands between his spread knees. He opens his eyes, staring at his alpha and friend. "What are they?"

"The male—"

"Who, the fanged one or the pretty one?" Cyrn smirks.

Ulric chuckles. "He's almost too handsome, yes?"

Cyrn thinks of the tall, hard male. Pale hair and eyes like cloud cover. "Not by our standards." First Species males are judged by a different standard entirely. One not just of looks but of prowess, fighting—power.

They look at each other, and finally Ulric nods. "Yes."

"He says his kind are called 'Reflectives.' Natural-born jumpers."

Cyrn pulls a confused face. "What?"

"You saw the female, how one minute she lay helpless and disabled on the field."

He nods, giving a significant glance to Ulric. "And the next she dangled off your weapon's belt…and committed the atrocity."

They are silent for a moment.

"Jeb Merrick is his name. He says they are soldiers."

"The woman also?" Cyrn asks, but he thinks he already knows the answer, judging by the throbbing of his face.

Ulric nods.

Cyrn lightly touches where she slapped him. Still stings. *Perhaps.* "She is so small." Cyrn has never seen a female so slight. But the look in her eyes is not delicate. It is hard.

Ulric's expression bleeds to neutrality, and he meets Cyrn's gaze dead-on. "Deadly."

He folds his arms, relaxing back in his seat. "Why are they here?"

"This Merrick claims they followed Beth Jasper here, because she was injured in a jump between one world to their world of origin."

"This is not where they are from."

"True"—Ulric chuckles at the ridiculousness of that—"but Merrick claims that to save her a second wound, he slowed the process of their transfer and, in so doing, lost control of the route."

"Very confusing, all of that. Give me a solid tether and the moon at my back anytime over this Pathway—"

"It is not a Pathway travel. Essentially, these Reflectives make their own pathway through objects that reflect. You remember the loot we've taken from the Fragment who dare enter our clan?"

Cyrn does. Very interesting artifacts.

"The items that show reflection—images. They're called mirrors. They are portals, of a sort, to these people."

Cyrn says suddenly, "The female threatens to leave before she is fully healed."

Ulric's grin flashes into existence again. "Merrick believes her violent act was a way to disallow our torture, harm, or imparting permanent damage on her person."

He laughs at Cyrn's expression. "I know, my friend—we would never harm a female. However, from what Merrick tells me, these Reflectives face extreme danger whenever they move through these mirrored surfaces and travel to another world."

"They can leave. We have nothing interesting to offer." *The sooner Beth leaves, the better.*

Ulric's shrewd eyes scan him. "She is not what you think. Beth was here by accident, paralyzed from a bullet remnant."

"Bullet?" Cyrn's brows meet, then he remembers the Fragment. "Ah yes, the small projectiles that fly out of the smoking weapons."

Ulric nods. "Yes. But these were specialized. They explode upon impact."

Cyrn scowls harder. "What deplorable male shot a female?"

"Not all believe as we do."

Cyrn's exhale is pure disgust. *He is aware.* Though the Band who live peaceably in their fortresses of wood are a fine example of males who *do* treat females well. Though their alliance with the First Species is uneasy, there is mutual respect. If only they could act together, perhaps they could extinguish the flame of the Fragment's existence forever.

"Merrick has not spoken with her yet." Ulric smirks, and Cyrn does as well. The male would have much to heal after they subdued him. "But he insists she acted to protect something they call The Cause, and whatever pathetic way of life they maintain in their home world. He didn't expound, though it sounds like harsh realities have hit their world hard, and they want to leave here safely, find their leader, then return to where they came from."

Something doesn't make sense. "Where is their leader?" Cyrn asks slowly.

Ulric swipes a palm over his head, and Cyrn notes he's in his human form, though it is harder to maintain than gorillan, which is the half form all First Species can maintain effortlessly.

"Merrick is keeping some things from me."

Cyrn gives a sage nod.

"But this much is sure. They are a ragged group who have not bathed, eaten, or rested in a handful of days. We can see them as guests, then they leave."

"Even the female?" Cyrn's voice is sharper than he intended, for he knows how Ulric's mind works.

Ulric slowly shakes his head, saying in a low voice, "Never the female."

Cyrn smiles.

15

Beth

Beth's eyelids fly open as a small noise wakes her.

As she rolls over on her side, the wounds of her body announce themselves, and she bites her lip to keep from groaning. She's so weak her head feels attached by a noodle. She touches the wound and finds the vaguest ropelike scar.

"Traveler," a female voice from the railing calls.

Beth blinks, assessing the woman. She is tall and well fashioned of bone, as they would say in Papilio. Intelligent, with an IQ of…Beth does not know. It escapes her.

She frowns. Also, the woman is not part of the primate species, yet she is. Her most unusual eyes are the lightest shade of brown that could still be classified as such. Her long dark hair spirals out of control to a narrow waist that swells to broad hips.

"I am Natasha, Ulric's mate."

Beth says nothing, but her eyes stumble over the tray in the taller woman's hands. Food piled high steams in lazy opaque spirals.

Her mouth waters at the sight and smells. Now that imminent danger has been avoided, the basic needs of water and food have reasserted themselves, and her concave stomach fairly whimpers with reproach.

She swallows the painful emptiness. "I am Reflective Beth Jasper."

Natasha's face takes on a vague smile, as though she is secretly amused by Beth's introduction.

Beth can't determine what language to use. She can speak passable Fragment—which is simply the archaic speech of both the sphere-dwellers and Clansmen—and remnants of Three in a crude combination. But this?

Beth is unsure for the first time in a foreign sector. She's studied the languages of all the sectors, going beyond what was needed, even learning much of their slang.

Now she's on fragile ground. Her training, for the first time, isn't offering Beth the confidence she's accustomed to, and she's weak as a kitten.

"I don't know what a Reflective is." The woman's eyes cast down shyly. "But I have brought food and drink."

"Thank you," Beth says then tenses as the woman draws nearer. She is quite tall and, Beth suspects, timid.

Natasha carefully places the tray on the edge of the bed, at the farthest point from where Beth sits.

Delicious smells assail Beth. Pheasant, berries, and a mixture of deep green vegetation lay a meter from her gnawing belly.

Beth keeps a wary gaze on Natasha, and with a hidden blade at her ankle, she extracts the weapon and uses the tip to carefully hook the edge of the tray and slowly slide it closer.

Natasha's eyes widen at the sight. "You are armed?"

Beth nods, giving a crooked smile. "Always."

"What are you?"

Beth's lips quirk higher. "A woman."

Irritation flickers across the other woman's features, and Beth has a momentary pang of regret. She really shouldn't bite the hand that feeds her.

"A Reflective is a soldier."

Natasha's mocha-colored skin puckers between her brows. "A soldier of what?"

"Worlds." Beth slaps her hand on a large pheasant portion, and by feel, she grabs the correct part and lifts it to her lips. After tearing off the meat with her teeth, she slowly chews, never taking her eyes from Natasha. She's almost dizzy from the heady fragrance of the meat and restrains the groan that tries to break free.

"I won't harm you," Natasha says with a puzzled smile, shaking her head.

Beth nearly chokes on her food. "You couldn't hurt me," and after a moment's pause, "but I won't be attacked, either," Beth says through her food. She gulps the entire load down and tears off more, taking sips of icy water between bites. Her belly begins to fill but cramps at the sudden consumption after being empty for so long.

Natasha sighs, her brows coming together, and she folds her arms underneath her breasts. "You are smaller than me."

Beth forgets she's eating, smiling through the juice of the berries she's crushed between her teeth. "I could take down two of your males at once." She lifts a shoulder, because it's of no consequence. She mentions it only for clarity.

Beth wants to leave here, acquire Rachett—and get the hades back to Papilio.

These other considerations—Jeb's binding to her, her existence—are secondary to The Cause.

Beth's people are depending on the few Reflectives who remain to save their way of life.

Natasha laughs, and the sound doesn't match her sultry voice. It's a high and bright tinkling. Contagious.

Beth smiles despite her recent circumstances, fatigue, and abating hunger.

"The Men of the Tree are fierce." Her pale amber eyes search Beth's.

"Is that what they call themselves?" Beth muses aloud. Because she's curious. Reflectives don't explore, they police. But Beth has always dreamed of a time when she didn't need to restore order but could be a part of foreign chaos as a visitor.

Natasha clearly begins to lose patience, crossing her arms and tilting her head. "You are a female, the same as me."

"I *am* female—I am *not* the same as you."

Natasha's hands fist. "You don't know what I've been through—who I am." Her voice has gone low with anger.

Beth's lips curl. "And the same can be said about myself."

They stare at each other.

Natasha throws her arms out, indicating the dwelling Beth eats within. "One of our males cured you; Cyrn saved your life."

Beth acknowledges her comment with a chin dip. "I thanked him for that."

Natasha crosses her arms. "You don't seem very grateful."

Beth sighs, swinging her legs around to the edge of the bed, and stands. Her head swims, and even though Beth slept soundly, she is weak, and the food has not had sufficient time to restore her strength. Which, in turn, makes her angry. Beth hates feeling vulnerable.

"You are not well." Natasha's eyebrows draw together, and she steps nearer.

"Stay where you are."

Natasha spreads her palms. "Why don't you trust me?" She looks stricken.

Beth tilts her head. "I don't know, might be because your males are so bossy and violent." She thinks of Cyrn. "And I was fed blood."

A distrustful expression overtakes her face. "You sound like you're Fragment."

"I hear your accent. You try to bury it, but I hear it." Beth lifts a shoulder. "So I speak as you do."

"I hate the sound of their words." Natasha's voice is soft—careful. The girl's pale brown eyes shine with unshed tears.

Beth sucks a deep inhale and coughs from the pain. Her ribs are still bruised but healed from the breaks.

Natasha doesn't see Beth's wince of pain because she speaks to her feet. "The Men of the Tree saved me from the Fragment. I will be forever grateful."

Beth straightens with an effort. "The Reflectives have repaired the damage caused by scientists from another world. They were allowing these criminals to roam free here—unpoliced—and you and other innocents were paying the price." Beth recites the words by rote.

However, the deep pain riding the girl's face makes Beth's stomach churn. Of course, that's what Beth was bred for. The curator of justice. All Reflectives are.

Until her timepiece is no more.

Shouting reaches their ears, breaking up the small and brittle communion.

Beth recognizes Jeb's resolute words:

"I *will* see her."

She knows that tone.

"Beth is not seeing males."

Natasha's eyes cut to Beth.

"I will cut out your tongue if I hear the word *no* one more time."

Beth leans over the railing, forgetting Natasha at her elbow, and nearly falls.

The height is so much greater than she knew, and her fingers cinch the round, smooth wood of the railing. The platform of wood encircling the two large coniferous trees is much higher than the sequence of Bloodling encampments.

Beth staggers backward, her back hitting the wall, and she ignores the pain of her stumble, slapping her palms against the rough feel of the wood beneath her fingers.

"Jeb!" she yells.

A scuffle, then a crash.

Jeb appears at the railing, balancing on the balls of his feet. His filthy uniform is no more, and a tightly bound deep brown tunic is cinched low at his hips, his bright gray eyes showcased like captured stars against all that brown leather. His gaze lands on her with the same intensity they've always possessed. Jeb's face and exposed body wear the healing marks of a severe beating.

Cyrn's behind him.

Natasha scatters, sprinting to the corner of the roughly four-by-four-meter room. Her eyes wide, she watches the males.

Cyrn shoves Jeb through the space between the railing and the low-slung roof.

Jeb dives gracefully, as though he wasn't pushed but jumped of his own volition.

Their eyes meet, and Beth's fill with tears, her relief at seeing her partner is that great. A person in this world who loves her, where none did before.

He whirls, facing the giant primate male, who still assumes a sort of half-gorilla, half-human form.

Beth takes him in for the unique specimen he is. She's still curious of their people but remembers Cyrn's disdainful treatment of her and maintains a wide berth.

"Get out," Cyrn says to Jeb, and they circle each other.

Beth leaves the wall behind and steps beside Jeb. "I feel well enough. Jeb, Slade, and I can leave. I've slept—I've eaten." She turns her head, giving a nod of thanks to Natasha, and her eyes return to sweep over Cyrn. *I've drunk your blood*, Beth does not say.

Beth's traitorous body chooses that moment to go wild with healing heat fueled by the food she's consumed, and she slumps. Jeb catches her, but a large hand swallows her bicep in his grip at the same time.

"Don't touch me," Beth says, her eyes rolling up to Cyrn's whiskey-colored ones. They spin like warm fire as they smolder at her.

Cyrn smiles. "I have done far more intimate things to you than this, Reflective Jasper." His voice is a rasp of velvet inside Beth, and every bit of the steel of her rebels against him.

Beth tries to jerk her arm away, but he yanks her to him instead.

She leans away from him, arcing backward.

Jeb snaps his fist into Cyrn's nose.

Then it happens, as Cyrn's naked hand slides from her borrowed clothes and encircles her exposed flesh.

Something inside Beth explodes. A shield of some inexplicable invisible material melts away as though open to an inferno, and everything she is, everything she was, is no more.

Shaken, Beth backs away, though it's the last thing she wants to do. She wants to lie on this male and couple with him. Deep shame sears through Beth.

Just like that, her timepiece has vanished and, with it, her reservations about Cyrn. Because he is the one.

The prophesied soul mate.

16

He will not lay hands on Beth.

Jeb punches the First Species' smug face. The male isn't expecting it yet rolls out of the strike neatly. Jeb's intended hit somewhat glances the target instead of being the sound tap he'd intended.

He moves in front of Beth protectively, but she skirts around Jeb, going toward Cyrn.

"No!" Jeb is sure Cyrn won't hurt her, but he needs to reflect them the hades out of here before anything else can delay them. Then there is the matter of Slade.

Beth moves beyond Jeb's reach, barreling into Cyrn.

Cyrn growls reactively, sees it's her, and his fangs lengthen as he grips her shoulders.

Jeb begins to move forward, his hands fisting.

She slides her arms around Cyrn's waist and hangs on, turning the side of her face and laying it against the huge male's chest.

Jeb stills.

The mute surprise overtaking the First Species' face would be funny if Jeb wasn't as shocked by Beth's actions as Cyrn.

What game is she playing? Whatever it is, maybe they can use it as a diversion to leave.

Sweat breaks out on Jeb's upper lip, and the urge to go to Beth and tear her away from Cyrn turns his guts. But he must extend trust. At the end of the day, Beth is his prophesied one—but she is also Reflective. The Cause is never far from their thoughts, and the Thirteenth threads through his brain.

Forsake not The Cause.

His soul might be promised to Beth, but his heart still believes in The Cause.

"What?" Cyrn pries Beth's arms from around him and pushes her gently away.

Jeb's shoulders slump in relief.

Cyrn's face darkens on Beth. "Do not—do whatever you were doing, female."

"Cyrn," Natasha says with ringing reproach, "Beth is weak from her physical trials. Maybe she needs something more."

Blood.

Jeb's eyes travel Beth, wondering if this could be so.

Cyrn points a finger at Beth. "That female needs nothing but a swift kick in her behind."

Jeb glares at the male while watching Beth's expression go from hard to hurt in a moment.

What has happened?

He looks between Beth and Cyrn, and a terrible thought begins to take shape. Could it be?

No.

Cyrn regards Beth with thinly veiled disgust. Natasha, who Jeb understands is Ulric's mate, stares also but with more compassion.

"Beth," Jeb says softly, facing her back. Her arms hang limply at her sides—he's never seen her appear more defeated.

Beth doesn't turn or indicate in any way that she's heard him.

Jeb finally unclenches his jaw. "Is it your timepiece?"

Beth gives a single jerking nod.

His heart sinks, then Beth turns and holds out her hand to him. Slowly, Jeb takes it, and Beth spins toward him, falling into his arms.

He crushes her to him, daring to hope.

What she says next slays him—elates.

"There are two, Jeb."

Jeb pulls away, searching her nearly black eyes as he cups her face. "Who?" For all his exterior show of calm, his heart hammers without mercy at his insides, battering. He notices a smudge of dirt across the bridge of her nose and a small bit of purple juice on her lush lower lip and he wants to kiss it off.

Jeb swallows. The breath he doesn't take swells, beginning to burn inside him, hurting the internal injuries he suffered at the hands of the First Species.

Cyrn strides to them, looming above Beth with a nasty disregard aimed at her like a weapon.

She reaches up, cradling his face. "It is you, Jeb Merrick."

Jeb's shoulders relax, that fiery breath releasing in a whoosh. *Thank Principle.* He tastes the relief, and it's the finest meal he's ever had—the sweetest wine he's drunk.

He's waited these past months, and while he thought it would be years for Beth to discover who would be her soul mate, it is now.

She crooks her finger, indicating he should draw closer while the huge First Species is at her back and Ulric's mate silently looks on.

His eyes run over a suspicious Cyrn, making certain he does not touch her as he bends nearly in half to lean in close to her mouth.

Jeb frowns at her secrecy.

Their cheeks mingle, and her lips tickle his ear as she whispers in a frequency too high for most beings to overhear, "Cyrn is the other."

Jeb's shock is too great to contain. He drops his hold on Beth, backing away, and Cyrn watches the interchange with far too much interest for Jeb's liking.

"What is this?" Cyrn asks in a hiss, splitting his attention between them with sharp eyes.

But Beth doesn't answer him.

Cyrn takes advantage of Jeb's distance and grabs her arm, giving her a small shake. "What is happening?" he growls. "You are a cold and distant female, impervious to your own safety, talking of policing and defending races you do not know, then you embrace me?" His eyes land on her with distrust and accusation. "Someone whom you abhor more than yourself." He hikes his chin, literally gazing down his sculpted nose at her.

Beth reaches up and touches his face. The gesture is clearly featherlight of a caress, but the giant male jerks his jaw out of reach, making a disdainful noise deep in his throat. "Stop your games, female."

Jeb's exhale is exhausted, grief-filled.

Ulric explained how they would look upon a woman who would attempt to take her own life.

The pink ribbon of scar tissue is a glossy stripe against Beth's neck.

Was it the blood she drank from Cyrn? Did that disrupt the timepiece prematurely? Or was destiny forcing Beth into a slot plotted by fate?

And *two* males? Unheard of. However, most Reflectives *are* male. Why would a female be the one to have two mates and not the reverse?

And what of Slade, who supposedly claims Beth?

At that opportune moment, Slade hops lightly over the rail, joining Beth's bloated and awkward confession, though Cyrn remains unaware of her changed mindset, thank Principle.

Slade's nostrils flare, and he looks first at Beth then Cyrn. "What has happened?"

"Beth's timepiece is no more," Jeb answers in a flat voice as his hands ache to hold her.

Slade's eyes meet Jeb's with obvious disbelief, and he puts his hands on his hips, giving the evil eye to Cyrn.

Jeb longs for the First Species' death. If Jeb were lightning, he would have already struck him.

"Who is it, hopper?" Slade glares, and for the first time, Jeb notices his skin cast is wrong, sallow with a greenish undertone.

Jeb can't share Beth—and he knows Slade doesn't understand just how bad the news is.

Jeb slowly looks at Cyrn.

"What?" he seethes at them all, his molten eyes of gold narrowing to slivers of flame.

How can he possibly be Beth's soul mate? He is foul of manner and temper. He is fanged, for the love of Principle. Cyrn is some kind of prime male-slash-humanoid—*ah*, what does it matter? There is no reasoning with any of it. The compulsion is Principle chosen. Reflectives are meant to be paired with another in just this fashion. Their unspoken reward for serving justice to the sectors.

Jeb pegs his hands on his hips, furiously trying to work through an alternate future. One where they leave, and though Cyrn is the one, Jeb might be sufficient. After all, where is the precedence for such a thing?

Jeb begins to pace in the space, now greatly cramped with three males of size and tense disposition.

Beth seems to sense Cyrn's low regard for her and lowers her chin. "It is nothing. My call to be Reflective is at an end."

The male makes a triumphant noise in the back of his throat. "Not so noble after all, female."

Slade scowls. "Beth *is* a noble female."

Jeb frowns when he notes the fine tremble of Slade's hand as he wipes sweat off his forehead.

Beth puts her face in her hands.

Slade's scowl deepens. "You do not know this female."

Cyrn plants his legs wide and tilts his chin up, lasering a stare that would incinerate most directly at the Bloodling. "I know enough."

Natasha walks over to where Beth stands and pats her on the shoulder. "I will attend you when we bathe and you get another night's rest. It was too much to wake up out of recuperative rest, receive me, then the males have come all at once." Ulric's mate lifts a shoulder. "It would be too much for anyone."

Cyrn snorts, and Natasha gifts him with a glare.

He meets her look head-on. "*I* will take her to the hot springs. No female will ever go alone again." He folds his arms, and his return stare dares her to counter his statement.

An image of a naked Beth floats to the surface of Jeb's brain with Cyrn only a few meters away. His reply is swift and simple. "No."

Cyrn's eyes slim on Jeb.

Slade lifts a palm. "I will carry the females to the ground. I am Bloodling. I can accompany them."

Jeb swipes a palm over his face. Bad to worse.

Cyrn turns to face Slade, and Jeb sees a vague, almost shadowy resemblance between them. He shakes his head, and the resemblance is gone.

"I am responsible for Natasha." He jerks a thumb at Beth. "And her as well."

Jeb notes he doesn't look happy about it.

Beth's chin stays tucked.

Jeb remembers how it feels to know she is his perfect other half. To feel lust and love intermingled seamlessly and not have those feelings reciprocated.

Until now.

But what if Beth had hated him regardless of his feelings for her? Just as Cyrn appears to dislike her? Where would that leave Jeb?

Bereft.

"Natasha," Cyrn calls to her, and she walks toward him. Cyrn's attention returns to him and Slade. "You are free to roam our clan now that Ulric does not see either of you as a threat. But you"—he points a finger at Slade—"will not touch the mate of my alpha."

He looks Jeb square in the eye with his troubling gaze of twin burning suns. "And I am responsible for this female"—he jerks his chin in Beth's direction—"until she leaves us."

Beth flinches when he says "female," but she doesn't comment.

She could take any number of barbed insults. She has, Jeb knows. But now that her soul mate has been revealed, it's entirely different.

Her utter silence is noteworthy. The quiet has the feeling of an eye within the storm.

Slade looks to Jeb, and Jeb can only exhale his frustration. He'll get Beth out of here. He's thankful she's eaten—he'd been quite vocal about it—since they had not let him see her until he insisted.

They move to the platform, and Cyrn suddenly pivots, hitting Jeb in the jaw. Jeb falls on his ass in an ungraceful pile of limbs. "That's for hitting me."

Jeb rises slowly, feeling ashamed he didn't see the blow coming, and gingerly moves his jaw side to side.

This is her other soul mate?

Beth comes to stand before Cyrn, her chin held high. "Do not hit my partner, First Species scum."

Jeb knows what that comment cost her. The fullness of the lie hits him as he readies himself. That storm analogy might just come to fruition.

"What will you do, worthless female?" Cyrn goads.

"This," Beth says in classic decoy, raising her hand, and predictably, Cyrn catches that tiny wrist.

Her other hand reaches for his crotch and twists hard between his legs.

Cyrn drops her hand and lands hard on his knees, howling then choking on pain Jeb is well aware of.

Beth leaps over his writhing form and up to the rail. Jeb and Slade join her.

Neither comment on the tears draining from her eyes.

Jeb knows he could never hurt her as she just did Cyrn. Even to save her.

As she just saved Cyrn, though he'll never know it.

"Wait!" Natasha screams, but they don't. Slade has Beth curled against his body, and Jeb allows it.

He can sense Slade's protection of her as he leaps after them, grabbing another tether.

Jeb's nostrils flare.

And beneath that, his sickness.

17

Beth

It brings Beth a level of physical pain to have inflicted an injury against her soul mate.

That and the fact that he hates her make Beth feel as if her rib cage has been torn open to reveal her slain and barely beating heart.

Slade's strong arms tighten around her as they fall to the next tether.

Beth twirls and falls, spins and leaps. Not by herself but held in the arms of a Bloodling from Sector One.

Jeb is close behind, doing the same but not with the same expert grace. He is not a Man of the Tree—First Species—or Bloodling. He is Reflective and learning to follow like the quick study he is.

Her tears leak like an undammed stream as her gaze meets Jeb's.

He swings closely behind her as she clings to Slade's thick neck.

Jeb gives a slight shake of his head, conveying much with the gesture.

Do not worry.
Things will right themselves.

And the last idea she believes Jeb communicates—*I am here.*

Beth stifles a sob, dipping her forehead against Slade.

She has never had the aching need of another as she has for Jeb Merrick, and Beth now has a degree of sympathy for the last few months that he's had to pine for her—and she was oblivious.

No longer.

The feeling of her guts being torn out because Cyrn has been cruelly chosen by fate—Principle ordained—steals her breath.

What will I do? It can't be possible she's drawn to them both. Beth must seek the face of The Cause.

If only she can immerse herself, can ignore the growing awareness of this male. Cyrn.

Gorilla shapeshifting vampire, Beth vaguely identifies.

Beth grits her teeth as Slade lands on a platform barely above the ground, hard.

He rolls them to his side in a clumsy toss, and she falls away from him.

Jeb's landing is better, and he hops once, then runs to a stop at the edge of the six-by-six-meter square of the battered wood launching and landing platform.

Beth turns to Slade, who continues to lie where he landed.

"Are you hurt, Tiny Frog?"

She stares at Slade, witnessing a horrible transformation. "No," she croaks, ignoring his tender nickname.

Beth crawls over to Slade. "What's this?" But Beth thinks she knows.

She and Jeb exchange a full glance.

Internal bleeding and what the Threes might call cancer—a now extinct disease in Papilio—appear to have taken over Slade's body. Open boils sprout with consistent patterns over skin that was a pearl gray just hours ago and now looks as though it has a green undertone beneath the sores of disease.

"What has happened?" Beth asks frantically.

"It's advancing," Jeb replies, and Beth looks up from her perch above Slade. "What?" She hopes his answer will not be what she fears.

"He can't travel, Beth. Jump."

Her eyes return to Slade, the giant Bloodling laid low. A sight she thought never to see. "Did you know?" she whispers.

Slade nods. "I suspected I was sicker than most. That the hopping was killing me."

"Why didn't you stay in One? Let Jeb go without you." More tears burn her eyes, dropping on Slade's leather tunic and leaving damp spots of sadness.

Only his eyes are bright—alive. The slick obsidian fire burns as always. "Because what I wanted was right here." Slade cups her face. Coughs. The inky blood inherent of his race splatters his chest.

"Slade!" Beth cries, gripping the stiff leather of his borrowed clothing.

"No, Tiny Frog. Do not mourn me. Your father awaits you in One. Jacky and Madeline as well." His eyes find Jeb's over her shoulder. "Jeb will care for you." That black gaze sweeps her face, lingering over her lips. "He is the one, yes?"

She reluctantly nods. "And Cyrn," Beth says, barely above a whisper.

Slade closes his eyes, and Beth is sure he's gone, but when he opens them, his life blazes within. "Come close, Beth Jasper."

Beth plants her palms on either side of Slade's head and bends over his large body, her chest hovering over his.

"Cyrn *will* love you, Tiny Frog."

Beth vigorously shakes her head, denying his words—his imminent death.

She just squeezed Cyrn's testicles to make sure he *never* loved her. To save the male destiny chose for her from what he does not want. To make her even more unforgivable. A female who takes her own life and hurts a male in his most tender of places *will* be hated.

Slade reaches his finger up and strokes her chin. "Many times, a male will resist what he wants most."

Beth stills, thinking on his words, while Jeb stands silently behind them. Slade had resisted her only to woo her later. Now he lies dying.

Because of her.

"Maybe there is something that could be done," Jeb says quietly from behind Beth.

Slade's gaze moves to Jeb. "Do you really think there is anything, hopper?"

Jeb sinks to his haunches, silent for a heartbeat, then answers, "No."

Slade nods. "In my bones, I knew there was not a way."

"Don't leave, Slade." Beth's breath hitches. Slade might have desired her, and she did not hold the same feelings, but he'd been her friend. Slade respected her.

"I cannot have you, Tiny Frog. Your timepiece has chosen another." He touches her breastbone with his chilled fingers, and Beth grabs his hand out of the air and presses the cool flesh against her cheek.

"I am sorry, Slade," Beth says, tears running between their laced fingers.

"No, do not be. My life has been better for your inclusion in it."

A great thump causes her and Merrick to turn.

Cyrn has arrived on the opposite side of the platform with Natasha. He has thunder in his eyes—directed at Beth.

"Jeb," Beth says, knowing she might have to fight her soul mate—male or not.

"Stay there, Beth."

Jeb rises slowly, squaring off with Cyrn.

No!

Beth spins around to reassure Slade—she'll protect him while he's vulnerable. Beth will not leave him while he lies dying.

And he is gone.

Grief swamps Beth's insides like sick flowing lava.

And rage.

Anger that Principle chose this prime species male—one that has only hate for her. That Slade's been taken because he did the very thing she was born to do.

That Jeb has to help her against Cyrn because two have been ordained rather than one.

She can't bear to lose Jeb.

Or Cyrn.

Beth carefully folds the dead Bloodling's hands over his body, thinking briefly that no one had been able to beat Slade while he was alive. Not Ryan, not his own people—no nightloper.

But reflecting did. The jumps killed him. Too many in too quick a succession. Seeing her safe had been more important than his life.

Slade was braver than she'd known.

Beth turns and faces Cyrn. He carefully sets Natasha on her feet. His silent perusal of her and Jeb gets Beth's blood pumping.

Not with excitement but fear.

He'll kill her now for how she injured him. And Jeb too. After all, he is not bound to her as she is to him.

Beth will sacrifice herself. If Cyrn kills her first, Jeb is released from his soul bond, and so is she.

With Cyrn.

The heartbeat's decision thumps, then Beth launches herself at Cyrn, dagger raised.

His smile should give her pause, but as he raises a slim pipe to his mouth, Beth's eyes seek reflection automatically—finding nothing.

Cyrn's cheeks go concave then suddenly puff out as he blows through the narrow tube.

A slender needle bursts from the tip, flying through the air without sheen, and pierces Beth's throat. She gurgles a cry, landing at his feet instead of on his body as planned.

Jeb hurtles toward them as Beth loses feeling in her limbs, numbness climbing to her shoulders and flooding over her chest. "What?" she gasps and chokes. She desperately wants to extract the needle sticking out of her throat. But no matter how much she commands her mind to pluck it out with her fingers, the creeping lack of feeling disallows it.

"Excellent suggestion, Natasha," Cyrn comments.

Beth cannot even blink, and strangled tears crawl out of her eyes.

Jeb lands beside her, his head hitting the platform and bouncing up once. His light gray eyes find hers.

Jeb's fingers creep across the platform, seeking hers.

Beth cannot move—speak. She has only her eyes to convey her feelings.

He is able to reach the pant leg of her torn and grimy uniform. Beth breathes in and out, in and out. Even that is a struggle. The serum must effect circulatory differently than muscle mass, or even now she'd be strangling on her own breaths.

Cyrn watches her dispassionately.

Oh Principle. Beth tries to explain about Slade—about the soul mate situation, her lips open, but no sound comes out. The paralysis appears to stop at voice box height.

A shout reaches them, and Cyrn steps over her body with precise deliberation.

Natasha kneels. "I am not sure what possessed you to hurt Cyrn—after a blood share." She rolls her eyes. "This drug will keep you still and allow rest for the next day and night and for you to be fully restored from your injuries. I will see you are bathed." Natasha gives Beth a large, genuine smile.

Beth rolls her terrified eyes toward Jeb's.

His gaze is just as frantic. She knows how he feels exactly. Neither can protect the other.

Beth strains, hearing a voice.

It's familiar, though still distant.

After much back and forth conversation, a new presence is revealed on the platform. Beth knows the gait of those boots.

The small hairs at her nape lift.

Could any bit of fate be so cruel?

"This is her." Cyrn jerks a thumb in Beth's direction. "Glad to be rid of her. Cowardly and violent. It is good she goes to her own world."

Beth's eyes swing up in her head, and Ryan smiles at her, upside down. She makes frantic sounds, but they sound like smothered chuckles.

"What is wrong with her?" Ryan asks Cyrn, frowning.

He lifts a shoulder. "We shot her with the stillness dart."

Ryan lifts a perfect blond brow.

Gooseflesh spreads over Beth's exposed skin, and Natasha raises an eyebrow, inspecting her closely. "Is something wrong, Beth?"

Yes! A corrupt Reflective that wishes Jeb and me dead is here—in our very presence.

Natasha cannot hear her internal scream for help.

Beth is gnawed with regret that she didn't take Ryan's life when it was offered. For the very first time, Beth damns The Cause.

"You are fortunate Ulric's guards recognized you as a Reflective like these two. Otherwise, you might have met up with one of us who do not think too highly of your kind." Cyrn gives Ryan hard eyes.

Ryan smiles disarmingly. "I apologize. This is your first introduction to Reflectives, and it's been a poor one. Both Merrick and Jasper are part of what has been named a Reflective Dissent and are wanted by the lawmen of our world."

Beth dies inside, her face heating with frustration.

"I don't know, Cyrn. Beth seems like she's trying to say something." Natasha frowns, appearing disquieted by Beth's every attempt to articulate their circumstance.

Ryan's smile is sly in response.

Beth begs Natasha with her eyes.

Jeb actually manages to lift a finger. His eyes are narrow slits of hate on Ryan.

Ryan presses his boot atop Jeb's hand, squashing his finger. "They are probably alarmed at me finally catching up with them. Criminals always are."

Cyrn looks from Beth to Jeb and finally to Ryan.

Beth's love for him swells, and the overpowering impulse to crawl to Cyrn and declare her feelings seizes her. Yet the serum keeps her immobile. The irony is painful.

"What of the Bloodling?" Ryan asks suddenly.

"We do not know. After the female nearly twisted my nuts from my body"—he gives Beth a dark look—"I was forced to recuperate, then I found them here and the Bloodling dead."

Ryan grasps his chin while Beth's lips burn with the desire to talk.

He walks to where Slade's body lies, and Beth manages a choked sound at the thought of Ryan desecrating her friend.

A male who fought for her. Loved her, though she could not reciprocate.

Beth watches Ryan toe his limp form. "Jumping sickness. Seen something like this before."

"It *is* unnatural." Cyrn nods toward Ryan then casts a lingering glance at Slade's body.

Ryan's grin is angelic. "Only for those not born to jump."

Cyrn says nothing, his brows dropping low over his beautiful gold eyes. "As you say." He turns to Natasha. "See to the female, and I will escort her to the hot springs momentarily."

Ryan jerks his head back, clenching his jaw. "I was hoping to take the Reflectives straight to Papilio."

Cyrn stares at Ryan.

Please, please, please grow suspicious, Cyrn, Beth thinks. *Hate me all you want, but don't let him have us.*

Ryan doesn't push. Instead, he takes his foot off Jeb's hand and leans over the side of the platform. He appears to spy something of interest. Beth interprets this easily from his loathsome expression of anticipatory excitement.

She sees the tread of Ryan's boot left on Jeb's palm.

"Good, a net's in place. I wondered how we'd get the two of them down—they're not unlike the Bloodling at present." Ryan chuckles.

Cyrn's guarded expression turns into a frown.

Ryan walks over to Jeb, and Beth's mouth falls open.

He wraps his strong hand around Jeb's forearm and drags him to the edge of the platform.

Jeb's wide eyes meet hers a nanosecond before Ryan tosses him over the edge.

Beth tries to scream, and nothing comes out.

Ryan turns, facing Beth.

"I don't like him," Natasha whispers to Beth, her eyes distrustfully flicking to Ryan.

Beth's eyes move to hers. *Help me!* her gaze screams.

Natasha looks to Cyrn, who in turn shifts his gaze at Ryan.

Beth sees the fine wheels of his shrewd mind spinning. Will he connect circumstance enough to help her and Jeb?

Ryan leans over her body, and a small whimper scrapes out of her from deep inside. His evil grin spreads on his face as he clamps the same hand that just surrounded her partner around her smaller forearm, yanking her across the platform.

Beth's body helplessly spins and flops at the rough treatment, new bruises forming over the healed wounds of a day ago.

She reaches the edge and catches a quick glimpse of Jeb hung like a fly in a web below them, and her neck tenses, the small muscles the only ones she can control.

Beth's upper body is suspended above the platform, ready to be shoved into the net to land on top of Jeb, and her eyes widen painfully as her vision fills with her partner—her newly discovered soul mate.

Suddenly, a strong arm latches onto Reflective Ryan, and corded tendons like muscled rubber bands stretch taut. "You will not throw her on top of the other Reflective or hurt her in any way, traveler."

Their eyes lock.

Beth knows that hers are wide and full of terror, and dirty tracks must mar the skin of her face from her tears.

And for only a split second, Cyrn sees her.

Sees her.

Beth's fear and desperation, her regret and apology rolled up into a silent final plea.

And in that moment, Beth sees *him*. More than her soul mate. The male underneath the mask.

A seed of tenderness is buried deeply within Cyrn.

For her.

Then it is gone, and she's tumbling over the edge, a silent scream entombed in her throat.

18

Cyrn

Cyrn growls as he leaps after the female, his hand grasping onto a tether not strong enough for his size.

He swings hard, anyway—Cyrn knows he can manage the fall. Thankfully, they were on the first platform.

It's the female he's worried about.

He did not like the look in her dark brown eyes. She fears this Reflective Ryan.

And any female brave enough to attack Cyrn the way she did, and with the skill Beth employed, would not be quick to feel fear.

Ulric will be told. And the Reflective will not be given any more latitude. He pushed the female off the platform after Cyrn expressly told him not to.

First Species do not harm females. They are the life bearers.

Beth tumbles beneath him, and the tether burns his flesh as he uses it to zip down in an inelegant fall of necessity. At the last moment of the plunge, he grips the tether while grabbing the female.

The twisted vegetation snaps tight, and Cyrn tenses, sure the too-small vine will snap with the momentum and weight of their combined load.

Her helpless body folds over his arm, dangling in a limp swing of limbs.

Cyrn smiles. She is a tiny female, but while in motion, she appears like the spinning cyclones of earth that tear through the open prairies outside their clan in the trees.

Carefully, he turns her over, keeping some distance in case the stillness drug wears and she attacks him again.

Wide, deep brown eyes caress his face with a relief so profound he feels moved. Then Cyrn remembers that she held his balls in her delicately capable hands.

His lips flatten. Cyrn will not hurt her, but he will not treat her with the same respect afforded females who do not batter a male who has fed them his very essence.

Perhaps this Reflective is correct—she and Jeb Merrick are dissenters and subject to their world's laws of crime.

Beth's eyes grow wide, and she says something.

With one arm, Cyrn lowers himself in a slow spin to the ground.

Jeb Merrick faces the ground, drool pooling underneath him as the net bites into the flesh of his face and neck.

"What?" Cyrn asks quietly.

"Murderer," Beth says, and her fingers twitch.

Cyrn feels his face scrunch; the stillness drug is already waning. "I would never harm a female. Even you." He scowls at her.

Ryan dumps to his feet close by. And Cyrn instinctively moves Beth out of the Reflective's reach.

"Ulric will not condone your treatment of the female." Cyrn flares his nostrils. First Species' sense of smell is extremely sensitive.

He smells the female's desolation and fear, and it burns his nostrils. Cyrn also smells this male Reflective's smug triumph.

Cyrn understands that if these two travelers—Reflectives—are truly criminals that were difficult to apprehend, then yes, there is a valid justice to having finally captured them.

But somehow, Cyrn senses something is off.

"Cyrn," Natasha calls from above them.

Damn. In all the trouble to protect this ungrateful female, he had left his Alpha's woman on the platform.

What is it about Beth that scrambles his otherwise cool thought processes?

He doesn't have time to process it all as First Species bleed out of the woods, including Ulric. "What has happened?" His eyes sweep to the first platform and see that his mate is unharmed and well, and his shoulders lower minutely.

Cyrn does not wish to discuss everything that just transpired. Not in front of Reflective Ryan.

"Everything is as it should be, except..." Cyrn glances down at the female Reflective, Beth. Her head is tucked inside the crook of his arm. She is so small he can almost hold her entire body in one arm.

Cyrn clamps his teeth together. He does not want to let her go, regardless of her lack of will to live. Her transgression in trying to unman him. There is something indefinable that causes him to tighten his hold.

He does not let on this subtle change of heart.

Beth's fingers curl around his arm, and he stares at them. Birdlike and slim, these are the digits that injured him.

She grips his arm. Cyrn watches her walk those fingers up to the neckline of his tunic. She clenches it.

"He," she breathes, swallowing hard.

At that moment, her partner rolls over so his face is toward the sky rather than smashed into the netting.

Jeb Merrick shouts, and the one word is enough to cause the First Species to spread wide and far.

"Traitor!"

Cyrn whirls too late as Ryan's hand buries in the female's hair. Fisting it tightly, Ryan pulls, jumping simultaneously.

A ribbon of iridescence slices the air, whipping particles of sparkling matter like a breakwater of floating dust motes.

Cyrn leaps forward, his arms swinging wildly through the tail of that glittering swath.

Merrick's hands rip the netting, and he falls through the tear face-first. Using only his hands to brace his fall, he lands hard, knocking the wind out of himself.

"Cyrn!" Ulric roars. "What is this?"

"The Reflective—he's taken the female."

Ulric sights Natasha again, ascertaining her well-being, and nods. "I gave him permission. He said she and the male were wanted for crimes against the government of their world."

Cyrn's desperate eyes seek Beth. She's vanished.

The male she is terrified of has her. And Beth can move only her hands—use her voice. She is helpless.

Merrick rolls over, groaning. "Can't let him take her," he wheezes, struggling through the relentless effects of the drug.

"Proof is not something I need. We rescued the female, and my Beta saw to her needs, giving her his essence. We need do no more," Ulric says reasonably.

"Follow her."

Merrick's eyes meet Cyrn.

"Will I die as the Bloodling?"

"I don't know. But if she is in Ryan's care for much longer, she will wish for death."

Cyrn's body tightens. He should have listened to his instincts. Maybe the words she attempted to utter were not for him but for Ryan.

Murderer.

Maybe *he* is the murderer. Or part of this so-called Reflective Dissent. Perhaps she was fleeing him and not the male who lies on the forest floor, regaining the feeling they robbed from him.

Perhaps they've misunderstood everything from the beginning.

Shame floods Cyrn. He did not listen to anything the female said. Assuming too much and ascertaining too little.

Now she is gone.

"How?" Cyrn asks, his long fingers moving into tight fists and staring at the male Reflective.

Ulric steps in front of him. "Are you considering interfering with their business when we have more than we can cope with here, in our own clan?"

Cyrn feels his Alpha's power wash over him, attempting to soothe his raw nerves.

Nothing works. His guts roil.

Cyrn is unmated. Beth Jasper is a foreign female who tried to take her own life. She attacked him. He reminds himself of all the points of why he should not interfere—care.

Beth moves him. Profoundly. He can't deny that. "The female is in danger."

"Cyrn," Ulric begins, sweeping his hand toward Merrick, "let the traveler—jumper, whatever they call themselves—deal with their own issues. We did our part."

Yes, they saved the Reflective female. True. But now she is gone, and the male who supposedly needed to be returned to their world writhes at their feet—forgotten.

"Ulric," Natasha calls from the platform.

His Alpha swiftly moves to the edge. "Come."

Natasha walks to the edge, her toes overhanging. Jumps.

Merrick's eyes widen as Ulric catches his mate with ease. First Species live in trees, and their limbs are aptly suited to maneuver all kinds of physical challenges.

And Cyrn's arms ache for the small female. But only to protect her, Cyrn tells himself. Once he is assured of her protection, he will release her.

"Time is wasting. Ryan could be doing anything," the Reflective says from the ground, though he attempts to stand.

Cyrn stares at the male. "How did he jump out of here?"

"We removed anything mirrored once we understood your capabilities."

Merrick stands. Falls. Tries again. Cyrn's exhale is impatient, and he strides to the shorter man and hauls him to his feet. They twist beneath him, and he begins to go down again.

Natasha is set on her feet, and she comes to them. "How long will this stillness last?"

She lifts a shoulder, her darkly kinked hair sliding over it. "Remember what Jim said?"

Cyrn did not, or he wouldn't be asking.

"That it depended on metabolism and race—gender—many factors," Ulric begins slowly.

Jim was a traveler from a world of thieves and debauchery. He had been a brave male to return to such a place. He had also left behind an assortment of useful items. The stillness drug was one. He had instructed them that if killing wasn't desired but incapacitation was—this was the trick. His words still rang in Cyrn's brain.

"The jumper—Reflective—he is worthless." Cyrn stares at Merrick.

"No," Merrick answers, his grip surprisingly strong at Cyrn's shoulder. "I can jump you in his tail, but *you* will have to help Beth. I am still too weak from this injection."

"She will kick my nuts in again." Cyrn feels the ghost of a smile form.

Merrick looks up at him, licking his parched lips. "I think she grabbed them." A faint smile creases his mouth, but his pale gray eyes have darkened with worry.

"This Reflective"—he swallows, coughs, continues—"he will hurt Beth first—then he will destroy our world."

Cyrn's brows meet, and a low growl breaks the seal of his lips.

Ulric touches his shoulder. "I cannot leave—this is you, Cyrn, and what you do next goes far beyond what even I would ask of you."

Cyrn nods and hauls the Reflective against him easily.

"What do you need?" Cyrn asks abruptly.

"Blade," Merrick gasps.

Ulric unsheathes a shining blade. Because dawn is so near, vague light seeks the metal, and a dull reflection sinks into the surface.

Cyrn sees very well at night, as most of the First Species cannot go out during daylight unless they are in full gorillan form. Gold and gray eyes pair on the dull surface.

Actually, Cyrn can make out only smears of color from their irises—no detail appears at all to his sight.

The Reflective takes a deep inhale. Releases.

Without warning, heat bursts from Cyrn's middle torso. Flames and ice bite down upon his arms and legs, bursting into a teeth-clenching sensation of being burned alive while simultaneously chilled to the bone.

The vision of Ulric before him narrows, and with an audible pop, he disappears. Cyrn twirls with the male Reflective, falling and spinning in a nauseating whirlpool sensation.

Whatever the magic is that allows the travel releases them, and Cyrn holds the Reflective tightly, reflexively throwing his arm out for a tether.

Finding none.

Cyrn tumbles in a free fall through trees. Branches tear at his sides, and with only one arm available, he grabs what he can.

A large branch slaps his ribs, breaking one. He grits his teeth and hits the branch with his arm.

The Reflective begins to slip, and with a shout of pain, Cyrn wraps his arm around the branch.

They bounce against the tree, and Cyrn's arm comes out of its socket.

Merrick and he swing on the branch, and Cyrn's pain is so great he doesn't waste breath with words.

The Reflective blinks, and they're suddenly sitting on the branch that broke Cyrn's rib and tore his shoulder out. Cyrn grabs the trunk with his good arm and locks his ankles around Merrick's torso.

"How," Cyrn gasps around the agony.

"Reflected us here."

Cyrn's eyes move up to where Jeb's gaze moves and see a mirror embedded in the tree above their heads.

"Ryan dropped it. Had to. It's how they got out of Thirteen."

Cyrn frowns.

"Your world."

Merrick stands, and Cyrn tenses. This is where the Reflective will kick him off the branch, and he will be helpless to do anything but die from the fall. There are no tethers wherever they've jumped to.

Instead he disappears and reappears within seconds.

With the small mirror in hand.

"We can go anywhere now."

"Do you still need me, Reflective?" Cyrn hates being at his mercy.

"No."

Then he grins, as though he knew exactly what Cyrn's thought process was. "Beth does."

Cyrn does not scream when the Reflective sets the joint of his arm.

19

Beth

Ryan dumps her on a cot, and Beth bounces, throwing out a hand to steady herself.

She's partially set to rights, being able to move her arms and legs, but bits and pieces remain numb.

He looms above her, his hands on his hips. Ryan's face holds a neutral expression that gradually turns into a grin.

"Looks like we're in Sector Seven, Jasper."

Beth blinks. She has jumped there, and though it's similar to Three in many respects, there are different factions in the works on this sector.

Fae. Vampire. Shifters.

Blood Singers.

"Why?" Beth asks in a hoarse croak. She clears her throat and tries again.

Ryan waffles his hand around. "Seemed like a good detour for Merrick to get lost in."

Oh no.

Beth attempts to sit up, and Ryan uses two fingers to press her flat against the cot.

Her heart rate trips, stuttering in fear. At any moment, Ryan will go ballistic, and she'll be at his mercy. The drug has made her powerless.

"Merrick has no Reflections," Beth tries.

He glares at her, and she shrinks away, his fingers digging into her sternum. "He'll find something. He's Reflective, if you've forgotten."

The fingers he uses begin to bruise.

Beth fights for air.

Suddenly, Ryan lifts his fingers.

She gasps, sucking in precious lungfuls of air.

Ryan walks across the dimly lit cabin, back to Beth, as he gazes out the filthy glass. "We wait here."

Beth manages to sit upright, and he whirls. "Don't try anything, Jasper, or I'll make everything I do to you go slow."

They stare at each other.

Beth's breaths come easier, and only one numb spot remains. "What are your plans?"

What she really wants to ask is why he hasn't killed her. Papilio is gradually being set to rights. Reflective Lance Ryan's on the run. Having her won't change that there's nowhere to go that he won't be pursued.

"I've made a deal with the devil."

A common Three expression, Beth thinks. But one that doesn't make sense in this context.

Why has Reflective Ryan jumped them to Sector Seven? Why are they inside a derelict cabin in the middle of nowhere?

His hands-off approach makes her very nervous. By this time, he'd be beating her.

And rape would follow. That's all that Ryan is capable of.

Yet he doesn't do those things.

He waits.

For whom?

"What are you saying? Because—you know there's no place you can hide. One hundred Reflective warriors have been returned to Papilio and will not rest until you've been brought to justice. Our females are being located—Papilio and the quadrants are being restored. You've lost, Ryan."

Beth tilts her chin up, and Ryan studies her face as though memorizing it. "I want to chew you up and spit you out, mongrel."

His eyes travel her form, and as filthy, haggard, and worn as she is—Ryan looks at her as if she's a juicy morsel.

"However, I'll restrain myself. If I am patient, and I will be, I can have everything I want. Madeline DeVere will be my mate." He fists his hand, pumping it along his hip in a vaguely lewd gesture. "You will be my whore."

"I will never be anything to you," Beth corrects him in a low voice.

He smiles, and his beautiful sea-blue eyes sparkle. And again, Beth is struck with how evil can wear such a handsome face.

"But first," he says, ignoring her words, "I will sell you to the highest bidder. Actually"—his grin stretches wider across his face—"I already have."

The air trembles around them, the vibration at once alarming and utterly familiar.

With an audible crackle, two images appear, and a jumping ribbon disturbs the dust in the air between Beth and Ryan and the wavering forms become solid.

Her beaten father and Maddie—a blade to her throat—appear, and Gunnar's eyes widen at the sight of her on the cot.

Next to him are three hyena nightlopers.

Beth stands and subtly drops what was in her hand. Jacky's words come back to her.

Trail of bread crumbs. Jeb will need this if he comes after her.

And if he feels for Beth even a minuscule amount of what she feels for him, he will.

Jeb Merrick will seek her.

"As I said, here she is." Ryan sweeps his palm toward Beth. "But I want what we bargained for." His brows come together, and he slides a locator out of his pocket.

Beth dies to see even a dot of reflection, but Ryan palms the entirety of the sphere.

Her shoulders slump.

The nightloper turns his slanted eyes toward Ryan. "If there is anything left." His voice is between a yip and a growl, and gooseflesh creeps over Beth.

Gunnar growls through his split lip, risking a glance at Beth.

Their eyes lock. His ebony gaze is desperate. Beth is sure hers looks the same.

Ryan lifts his head, his expression subtly mocking. "If you want her to produce, you'll have to keep her healthy."

The half-formed hyena looks at Beth, and his amber eyes, not unlike Cyrn's but cold as ice, stare her down.

His intent is as clear as if he'd spoken it.

Beth's body chills from his expression.

All of what she is, what Slade had told her, comes back to her.

The nightlopers have sheer numbers. They were, in comparison, mindless predators and, thankfully, without any jumping ability of their own.

Unless they were to get their hands on a female Reflective. Which, thus far, has not been possible. Before Ryan's revolt and uprising of the dissenters, the female Reflectives had been heavily guarded. Except for Beth.

She had been a soldier.

The nightloper tosses Maddie toward Ryan, who catches her easily. Maddie screams for Gunnar, and he roars.

Ryan flashes to Beth, tossing her to Gunnar, who reflexively catches her.

The ceramic blade abrades the healing scar at her throat as the hyena's foul breath bathes her face.

Ryan strokes Maddie's hair, and she whimpers in fear. Her wide, beautiful violet-blue eyes implore Gunnar, and Beth can sense how sick he is not to protect her.

"Take the Bloodling and the female back to One. I'll be in touch—after I get acquainted with my new bride— and correct what's been done to my home world."

The nightlopers whistle an ascending note.

Gunnar jumps them. What can he do when a blade is to his daughter's throat?

A reflection has never felt so wrong.

Jeb hurries, jogging fast through the brush after Cyrn.

They don't have time for testosterone, hysterics, or drama. Jeb and Slade had not gotten along, and now he is dead.

Cyrn is very different, having shown Beth not a shred of deference, aside from feeding her his blood under command from Ulric.

Now Reflective Ryan has her, and questions plague Jeb as to why.

He should kill Beth. Ryan is being actively hunted. There isn't a safe sector to jump to where he will not be sought.

Except this one.

Sector Seven has its issues but none that require Reflective interference—yet. That Ryan has chosen to jump here is savvy. He came to the sector Reflectives don't normally man and where they would not think to seek him.

Does he hope to hide here? And if so, why take Beth? He could have killed her outright and been done with them. He hadn't even tried for Jeb—though with the serum, they'd been easy pickings. Ryan could have murdered them both and fled before the First Species could have retaliated. Even if they wanted to. Ulric had been forthcoming about their aversion with trifling in the affairs of outsiders. If it wasn't an issue for his clan, they stayed out of it.

The only reason they'd seen to Beth was because she was female. Ulric told Jeb a male would have been left to die—or worse, suffer the Fragment's devices.

Cyrn leaps from tree branch to tree branch easily. Jeb is amazed he can gauge the readiness of the branches for his weight. Somehow, he does.

The male suddenly drops only three meters from Jeb and turns. He jerks his jaw at a remote, dilapidated cabin that sits on a knoll inside a small clearing.

"I scent them both."

Jeb could sense Beth but not Ryan. The soul bond has to be the reason. And now that she was linked to Jeb, she could likewise sense him.

Jeb's eyes move to Cyrn. And the First Species. Who remains blissfully unaware of his role.

That he would feel any obligation to help Beth is a mystery to Jeb. Now that the jump has healed Jeb of his injuries—but still the disquieting numbness remained in some parts of his body—he didn't expressly need the hulking male.

But if he wanted to sacrifice himself so Jeb could get Beth to safety? That was fine by him. Doubly fine, considering the big male was the other part of her soul mate equation.

Just as they creep up the hill, Jeb feels the telltale heat of precipitating a jump.

He breaks into a sprint and throws open a small wooden door hanging on by only one latch.

Beth's essence is everywhere. Jeb can't lock in on it.

There are two tailwinds.

Cyrn crashes through the doorway, scraping the door's bottom so hard against the floor that it splits the wood.

"Where?" he shouts.

Jeb sees nothing but iridescent dust motes. He grabs a handful out of the air. They mix, and he shouts in frustration.

"Don't know."

Jeb whips his face around, looking for any clue, and sees something small on the floor.

The emblem of The Cause rests on the dirty wide-plank wooden floor. Jeb scoops it up and crushes the piece of embroidered material in his hand.

"What is it?" Cyrn asks.

"Beth was here."

He scowls, searching the room again. "She is gone."

Jeb nods.

"We'll have to split up—I don't know which direction she took. I can't read her signal because it's mixed up with two simultaneous jumps."

"What does that mean?"

Jeb stares at the foreign warrior. A male who on another planet could be classified as myth—legend.

The tailwind of their jump is fading. Jeb must act quickly.

"I will jump you on one tail, and I will jump the other."

"Where will I go?"

Jeb shrugs. "I do not know."

Cyrn glares at Jeb. "How will I return?"

This is the hardest part. The most honest. Jeb swallows, damning the First Species.

"You don't."

The silence has its own presence. Weight.

Finally, Cyrn nods his acquiescence.

Jeb grips his shoulder, lifting the mirror.

Heat sears them, and Jeb shoves the opposite coordinates at Cyrn. Toward what he is at a molecular level, directing that spinning, invisible mass in one direction, to an unknown sector.

Jeb jumps to the other.

The End

Reflection #4, coming in 2017!

Directives of The Cause:

First: *Right the wrong*
Second: *Bear no injustice*
Third: *Change not what must be*
Fourth: *Reflect only when unobserved*
Fifth: *Protect the young*
Sixth: *Take life only in defense of another*
Seventh: *No death is without consequence*
Eighth: *Defend those who cannot*
Ninth: *Forsake not honor, for it is all that remains*
Tenth: *Reconcile emotion for The Cause, not another*
Eleventh: *Divulge not your identity*
Twelfth: *Disturb not the continuum*
Thirteenth: *Forsake not The Cause*

Sectors:

Sector One – Nightloper/Bloodlings
Sector Three - Earth
Sector Seven - Blood Singers
Sector Ten - Papilio
Sector Thirteen - Spheres

Unexplored Sectors:

Two
Four through Six
Eight
Nine
Eleven
Twelve

Please read on for a dark romance sample by Marata Eros, a pen name for Tamara Rose Blodgett.

NOOSE

NEW YORK TIMES BESTSELLING AUTHOR
MARATA EROS

All Rights Reserved.
Copyright © 2016 Marata Eros

This book is a work of fiction. The names, characters, places, and incidents are products of the writer's imagination or have been used fictitiously and are not to be construed as real. Any resemblance to persons, living or dead, actual events, locales or organizations is entirely coincidental.

This book is licensed for your personal enjoyment only. This ebook may not be re-sold or given away to other people. If you would like to share this book with another person, please purchase an additional copy for each recipient. If you're reading this book and did not purchase it, or it was not purchased for your use only, then please return to a legitimate retailer and purchase your own copy. Thank you for respecting the hard work of this author.

Marata Eros Website: *http://marataeroseroticaauthor.blogspot.com/*

Marata Eros FB Fan Page: *https://www.facebook.com/pages/Marata-Eros/336334243087970*

Cover art by **Willsin Rowe**

Editing suggestions provided by **Red Adept Editing.**

SYNOPSIS

Whores
A smorgasbord of sweet butts, one for every taste.

Noose has a sweet tooth that won't quit, and a clubwhore to suit his every need.

Being a part of the Road Kill Motorcycle Club isn't a hard choice for Noose. A former Navy Seal and expert knotter, he's seen realtime choices—in circumstances most never do.

It's killing road. Women and freedom are the benefits of being a one percenter.

Until Rose Christo comes along and slams the brakes on his outlaw existence.

Murderers
Rose Christo knows death.

Murder stole her sister, and gave her a son that's not hers.

Love doesn't come in neat packages; it comes in the form of a five-year-old boy.

Love is packaged in a man that tears out her heart with a brutal sexuality that strips Rose of her most sacred vow.

Never count on a man.

Never love.

Never.

When her sister's murderer comes calling, demanding his property, who does Rose trust?

1

NOOSE

I grab Crystal's hair, fisting it tightly against the scalp, and drive into her hard from behind.

She squeals, and I suck up the noise like a starving man.

Sweet butts are all the same. They want to be taken.

I want to take.

I love bareback, but rubbers are key. This pussy has had more dicks than I can count, and it's like fucking another man if you're not wearing a raincoat.

Even when it's not raining.

I'm done being introspective. I don't have to be anymore. I just fuck. I wear a rubber so I can fuck and not think.

Perfection.

Like the knots I make. Like the ones I've made to murder with.

Crystal moans.

I thrust harder and start swirling my dick high in a semi-circle. She screams, her cunt squeezing my dick in big deep pulses.

My balls get ready for lift-off, and I come from my toenails, emptying the double barrel right on target.

My head tips back, and I give an exhausted exhale.

When I finally come down, I slap her tight ass and withdraw, stripping the spent rubber from the top and rolling it off as I walk. Chucking the limp sheath in the trash can, I turn around. She's still there, tits still mounded on the tabletop I pushed her on, pussy all bright pink and plump.

Splayed for the next guy. If any were dumb enough to enter my lair. I smirk. *They sure as fuck shouldn't be.*

An exhale drives out of me, and I tear calloused fingers through my hair, wanting a smoke bad.

I glance again at Crystal's slit. It's a shame when a perfectly good pussy isn't leaking cum. I shake my head in partial regret.

Can't have it all.

Her head pops off the table, and she moves to the side, her natural large rack sort of rolling toward the tabletop. Crystal puts her head in her palm, studying me.

I admire the view as I hop into my jeans. Commando. I'll figure out underwear when she's outta here and I can grab a shower. For now, I just want to get my ass covered and have my post-coital drag.

NOOSE

I rummage through shit on the top of my battered chest of drawers and spy the hard box of cigs underneath a pair of clean underwear.

Snapping open the lid, I give the pack a wrist flick, and three cigarettes slide out. I open my lips and nip one out.

After flipping the lid closed, I toss the pack back on the dresser. I grab the lighter out of my jeans pocket and light up. Cupping my hand around the flame, I take the first drag then shoot a smoke ring toward the peeling paint of the graying ceiling.

Relief washes over me. I got off, time for a kick back, then I go back to work. I'm already hashing shit out for the day in my head when Crystal starts talking.

I'd forgotten she was there.

Her lips purse. Some girls think pouting is cute. *I* know it's the cue for a potential mega-rant in my near future.

Not having that noise.

She runs her hand through her bleached-blond hair, puffing it out on the side that was mashed against the tabletop.

My lips quirk. Her effort to be sexy is sort of fun, like free entertainment.

"Hey, baby, let me stay for a while," she says in a voice that tries too hard for bedroom smooth, finger trailing over her tit and tweaking the nipple.

Nice. I clamp the cig between my lips and shake my head. "Nope. Out." My thumb slings toward the bedroom door.

The big pout ensues, full bottom-lip treatment. "But"—she sits up, tits jiggling, and starts to walk fast after me—"I thought we could—"

"Nope," I repeat, flicking ash toward the ashtray as I stride toward the bathroom. Most of the inch-long ash lands in the glass bottom that reads Road Kill MC. How's that shit for propaganda? The Prez believes in the club like the Holy Grail.

I do too. It's all there is for us one percenters.

It's the road. The bike. And the women. Not always in that order. I don't need anything more than that. I never have.

I turn around fast, and Crystal bounces into my chest. My hand rests against the doorjamb leading into the bathroom. "Listen, you're cute." I give her chin a little chuck. "But I'm not looking for anything long-term." I lift my shoulder, blowing another lazy oval toward the ceiling.

Crystal looks ready to cry. God *damn.*

I stuff my cig in the ashtray, mashing it in half. Spirals of smoke curl upward. Grabbing my wallet off the nightstand beside the door, I jerk out two twenties and a ten.

I shove them at Crystal.

"Go buy yourself something hot. Something that shows tits and ass." Chicks like to shop. *What do they call it? Oh yeah—retail therapy.*

She grabs the money, looks down at it for a second, then throws it in my face. "I'm not a whore!"

I wince. The green bills floats to the worn carpet. *Act like a whore, look like a whore…*

"You're a sweet butt. And you *were* sweet." *Not so much now.* "But it's time for you to take off."

Her face reddens. "You're a jerk, Noose."

I've been called worse.

I step into the bathroom. I don't look at the sweet butt picking up the crumpled cash.

I kick the door closed behind me then give a hard turn to the faucet.

When the entire bathroom is steaming, I get inside the shower.

She'll be gone when I get out.

They always are.

I should have done my sets before I showered.

But no way was I going to have Crystal around while I work my shit out.

Tonight I'll do pushups, twisted sisters, and burpies until the cows come home.

There's always the punching bag. Nobody's ever using it when I come in. My fists will tire me out.

Fucking insomnia. The witching hour is officially mine. I own it.

I owned it over in Afghanistan too. Can't sleep when you know someone might kill you.

Or you might have to be the one doing the killing.

I move through the club with a lot of stealth, considering my size. It's part of why I was never a jumper in the military. Big guys get fucked up fast.

Six feet, four and two hundred twenty pounds of male has all kinds of potential for getting broken to bits. "The bigger they are, the harder they fall" has new meaning in a parachute.

That's why hands-on assassinations are so much more appealing.

Knots.

When I'm stressed out, my mind does them. My hands are restless to feel ropes under my fingertips—the abrasive kind or the slick new style that knots faster than my mind can think it.

I pass the kitchen, a hangman's knot wrapping my thoughts. The loop's perfectly symmetrical, winding and wrapping until there's a little loop, then I pull through—

"Noose!"

A rough hand claps my back, and I frown. *'Bout had that knot.* My favorite. Hence the namesake, I guess.

My team would know why, even though the club guys don't. They're probably under the impression it's a tough name or that it's cool.

It's not. Noose has meaning. But to those of us who fought side by side, we don't talk about obvious shit.

Our time just was.

NOOSE

I give a broad smile. Lots of us brothers have similar names.

Take Snare, the guy who's just put his hand on me. He gets out of those—traps, close calls, the works. The dude's got nine lives.

Nothing like a cat, though.

He lifts his fist, and I bump my knuckles with his. "Hey, man."

"Saw Crystal go outta here in a huff." His eyes, a blue so pale that they're the color of frozen water, hold humor. Snare's about three inches shorter than I am, but he's built like a brick shithouse.

I shrug at his words.

"How was she?" His eyes are hooded. He's probably thinking about the platter of pussy we have strutting around all the time. He hasn't sampled the Crystal hors d'oeuvre yet.

I lift my shoulder. "Same as the rest."

His eyebrows jerk in surprise. Snare's got some Native American in him. His hair's jet black. White folk never get hair that dark without help. The mix of light-blue eyes and black hair is striking—or so the ladies seem to think.

My hair is shit dishwater. Can't make up its mind between brown and blond. That doesn't matter; I keep the sides short and the top long. When it gets in my way, the whole load gets tied down.

Since I'm on the back of the bike half my waking hours, hair's tied down a fuckton.

I even have a little invisible hair tie for the beard. I keep that long and square. It's darker than the hair on my head, with a touch of ginger. Had a sweet butt ask me last month if I was Scottish.

Fuck if I know.

I guess I'm American, for what that's worth.

I'm a mad bastard, I told her. Then I went to town on her twat. That shut up the questions in a hurry. Just a lot of moaning and shit after.

That's how I like it—don't ask me for history.

"Come on, Noose, she's always pining for you. I haven't had a crack at her."

I chuckle. "Nice choice of words, bro."

He flings his muscular arms wide. "Not just another pretty face." Snare winks.

His face is not pretty. Snare got some blade time and a close call that almost took out his eyeball. The twisted scar tissue bisects one eyebrow, narrowly misses his eye, and travels in a hooked line that ends at the cleft of his chin.

Some girls are shy about Snare.

I think scars add character, though. It makes him look bad ass, which, in turn, freaks out the chicks. *Love/hate thing. Not bad for the sack.*

I exhale. "Crystal doesn't pine. She whines."

"Now who's the poet and they don't know it?" Snare asks, glacial eyes widening.

I flip him the bird. "Ass."

He nods. "Yup. But put in a good word for me anyways."

I give a lopsided grin. "I don't think Crystal's gonna think *any* of my words are good after our interlude."

Snare whistles, walking outside with me.

Brilliant sunlight belts me in the face, and I flick my sunglasses open. They're high-end and polarized. I don't like glare when I ride.

I slide them on my face, loving the anticipation of the wide-open ribbon of black asphalt.

"Interlude?" he asks in disbelief.

I throw up a hand and waffle it around. "Pelvic grind, hip bump, pipe lay…"

Snare grunts. "You ever done anyone twice, Noose?"

I narrow my gaze at him behind my dark glasses. "Nah."

"Figured."

Our attention turns to our rides. The windshields glint in the sun like sleepy, winking eyes.

"Let's ride," I say.

Snare doesn't need another invitation.

2

ROSE

It's my break.

I'm allowed to look at my text messages. I have to.

Charlie will send me pictures. He always does. *The sweetheart.*

I move through the breakroom, my hip hitting the countertop of the little kitchenette.

I grimace but hardly notice. A ping sounds, and an image fills my cell screen.

It's a Lego tower. A perfect, brilliant work of art.

For a five-year-old.

I smile like I just saw an original Picasso. Love swells my chest, and pride tightens it.

He's done *so* well.

"Hey, Rose," one of the other tellers greets me as she walks by.

"Hey, Naomi," I reply absently, brushing away a stray hair that's come loose from my topknot. My eyes are all

NOOSE

for the new little creation my boy made during his first week of kindergarten.

My heart flutters. I cried ten gallons of tears last week when I had to send him off. My sadness had been evil.

I guess all mothers feel that way. I don't know for sure. I'm not really a mom.

I'm an aunt.

But his real mom's dead. So I'll have to do.

I bite my lip, rolling the plump flesh inside my mouth and gnawing at it. My finger runs over the colorful blocks with a loving touch, my screen magnifies, and I see his left hand clutched over the top. A tower almost as tall as he is threatens to topple, but not before the teacher got the pic.

I text back rapidly. "Beautiful."

There's no return text.

I glance at the time on my cell. Naptime.

My heartbeat regains its slow rhythm. I try to overcome the panic at not immediately hearing back from him. I'm sort of a gloom-and-doom type.

I haven't seen Charlie's father in a year. *The fucking loser.*

Time feels pregnant with potential, swollen with his promise of getting his son back.

Over my dead body.

"Rose."

I know that voice and sigh. I lift my chin, meeting his gaze.

My boss stands there, his eyes steady on the clock over my left shoulder.

One minute past break.

Ned's about ten years older than I am. That puts him around thirty-four. He's married. Not that the little fact of his status as *taken* stops him from making passes at me whenever he can.

Ned found out fast that I don't date.

Ever.

I sure as hell don't date married men who are my boss.

Some of the girls don't care that he's married. They rise in the ranks faster for blowing him in his office. I've been a teller at this bank since high school graduation. My first boss died of a heart attack last year. Orville was a good man.

Now Ned's here.

He smirks, obviously enjoying the discovery of my minor transgression.

I slide off the stool, realizing I missed having a snack. Not great for the old hypoglycemia. *Stupid, Rose.* Oh well, maybe I can pop an M&M or two at my station.

He leans down next to my face as I pass him, his hot breath singeing my temple. "Don't let it happen again."

Sacrificing my body's natural aversion to a man, I try not to jerk away. I feel an expression of disgust seat itself on my face as I regard him.

His beady brown eyes slim on me with a hate that I don't deserve. Just because I say *no* doesn't mean I suck.

But to Ned, my lack of interest means exactly that.

I turn away quickly, trying to pretend those interchanges don't bug me or make me nervous.

That's crap, of course. Anxious sweat stings my palms and breaks out underneath my armpits. I hate feeling stressed where I work. My fingers curl around the cell.

I have Charlie.

I have a job. I have a hell of a lot to be thankful for. Crying over my perv boss like a scared little bitch won't solve it.

I just won't be late anymore. Even a minute. A second. I don't want to give the jerk anything to have over me.

I scoot my stool with the rolling wheels underneath the counter and lift my sign that says Next Window.

I'm ready to take money now.

I hate my boobs.

Other women think I've got it made or something. I fill out clothes nice, sure. But I have to wear two sports bras so the girls don't drive me crazy with bouncing. Besides, it kind of hurts if I don't.

Like now.

I jog around nine-minute miles most days. On the weekends, I go a little nuts and do around six-mile runs, then I'm a true jogger, slowing down too just under tens. During the week, between my job and Charlie, I can only manage around three times a week. I take Sundays off. That's Charlie's day.

My day.

I swear I live at Scenic Park. Rumor has it we had a mayor back in the 1970s who was out of control for parks and threw one in everywhere there was land.

Kent needs it. The city's a little armpit bedroom community to Seattle now. Infrastructure was not well thought out, and the traffic is a rat's nest of too many cars in clogged arteries. The roads of Kent have cholesterol, and there's not a damn thing we can do to stop the impending heart attack.

The valley bisects the east and west hills of the city. Kent's got long fingers of ownership that travel all the way to Federal Way to the west, cutting a path through that town and still claiming a narrow swath that belongs to the City of Kent.

I don't care about the impractical parks that could have been made into more roads or wider ones. I just like to jog the paths of Scenic Park and have a free, safe place to hang with my nephew.

The ritual of running erases my mind's problems and takes me on a journey of the soul without introspection. I can*not* think for that hour I'm pounding paths that wind through trees.

I don't think about my creeper boss. I don't think about Charlie's real dad, my sister's murderer.

I just run.

NOOSE

Charlie loves the park. If the wind's strong, we fly kites that get caught in the Douglas fir trees, tails like rainbow arcs toss their color in the deep blue of summer that comes late in the Pacific Northwest.

A wave of light-headedness washes over me, making my stride stutter.

Dammit.

My little waist pouch taps my hip softly as I run. I hate stopping the rhythm I set when I run. My sports watch says I was doing high eights. That's pretty fast for my slow ass. A tight smile stretches my lips. Just one more quarter mile, and my car will be in sight.

I can make it.

I take the last bit of my run hard, seeing what I've got left.

When my little Smartcar comes into sight I slow to a walk, cruising right past the shiny white toaster.

I'm begging to puke if I just stop and hop in. Nope. First, it's the ten-minute cool-down walk, then it's stretching.

First things first. I spring a Jolly Rancher candy free of my little pouch, tear off the wrapper, and stuff it inside my mouth, striding back and forth.

I probably look like a crazy pacer. I suck hard through my nose and breathe out my mouth, controlling my air. Sweet and sour apple flavor explodes inside my mouth as I suck on the candy, willing it to settle me and ground my fuzzy brain.

Being tied to protein and ready sugars gets old, but it could be worse. *Oh well.*

My tongue rolls the candy around in my mouth, my heartbeats slow, and my shakiness subsides.

I plant my hands at my hips, elbows out, and walk with my head down.

Back and forth, back and forth. I don't see, hear, or think.

I crunch my candy and cool down. That's probably why I didn't notice him at first.

Drake moves into my path.

I stop as if I just walked into an invisible wall. It sure feels like I did.

The wings of my elbows fold, and that heartbeat I had under control riots inside a chest that suddenly doesn't feel like taking in air.

"Hello, Rose."

He's just as I remember him from last year. Huge. Greasy. Sinister.

Dangerous.

I don't reply, pivoting quickly. I move to my car.

He's so fast, his hand is on the handle before I touch it.

I make a little noise of distress.

God, please.

Please.

His smile is cruel as he grits out, "We're gonna talk, bitch."

My heart flies up my throat. I try to reply but can't.

His hand grips my bicep, fingers biting the tender flesh just above the elbow.

"There's witnesses, Drake." I'm so proud of the evenness of my voice.

He nods. "I know that. We're gonna talk. Here. Now."

I swallow, craning my neck to get a good look at him. He's over six feet to my five feet, seven. His biker gang tats are all over him. The only tat-free space on his big body is his face. He reeks like body odor and ashtrays. Underneath that is pure evil.

I shudder.

His smile widens. He's so pleased by the effect he has on me, and I'm helpless to *not* react. Drake is the most repugnant man I've ever met in the flesh.

He drops my arm as though it burns him. I know that's not the case. He's told me I look as good as my sister. When he said that, tears burst from my eyeballs. Not a few. A flood.

He laughed.

The leather of his motorcycle jacket creaks when he shifts his weight. "Hearing's coming up."

I know that. I've lived knowing that.

My feet take me a few steps out of his reach. "I know."

"They're going to give me my boy back." A slow, false grin spreads on his face.

I shake my head, my lips thinning. "They'll take one look at you and give me another five years."

"You fucking *bitch*. Give me visitation rights."

I swallow my fear, as his hands become flesh hammers at his side.

"What rights?" I whisper in a choked voice, my fingers splaying over my heart. "What rights did Anna have?"

"She stepped out on me," Drake says, crossing his arms over his steroid-muscled chest.

"She *walked* out on you. Big difference. But if that helps you sleep at night…"

His eyes slim down on me. "I sleep like a baby." He puts a *V* around his lips and his tongue punches out. Wagging at me.

Disgust ripples through me. "What are you? Twelve?"

I shake my head, turning to walk back to my car. Defeated.

I have to see this maniac again in a week. I should have known he couldn't wait until then.

He reaches out, snagging my wrist. He grinds the small bones together. "You *will* say you're willing to give me visitation, or I'll make it so you wished you had."

A whimper slips out.

Drake likes the noise. His hold tightens slightly, then he drops my arm.

I fight not to rub my wrist.

I feel tears burn my eyes, knowing what my sister went through before she died. A taste of Drake's abuse is enough to last me a lifetime.

"You can't force me. Charlie's all I have of Anna. He's a human being, not a pawn for your control."

His thumb hits his chest. "He's my fucking kid. Unless that crack was fucking someone I don't know about?" His dark eyebrows twitch upward.

I wish she had.

But Charlie is all his. Anna had only just started dating another guy when she was murdered. Who knows if she ever slept with him? Charlie was already here, so it's a moot point.

Drake was the only man Anna slept with, as far as I know.

I shake my head.

He lifts his shoulders hard, driving them to his ears. Heavy gauges distend the lobes. They're jet black, like his clothes.

Like his heart.

"I'll be there." I jerk the handle up and heave myself inside, slamming the door.

Drake strides to the window and gives a single hard rap of his knuckles against the glass.

I flinch.

Starting the car, I crack the window.

"It's not you being there that matters. It's you vouching for me, cunt."

I hate that word. It's so dirty from his mouth.

I'm more than the sum of my parts. Ineffectual rage blossoms like a dark flower inside me, swarming my body with heat.

His lips twist savagely. "Yeah. I see how you are. What you'd like to do to me. But you can't. I'm in control, see?"

I do see, but I won't be manipulated. This won't stop. If I cave to Drake's demands, he won't stop there. He'll want more.

He won't stop until he has Charlie.

I can't let that happen.

His grimy fingers curl over the window rim.

I slam the gear in reverse and take off.

Drake snatches his hand away.

His glare haunts me even after he's out of sight.

Available wherever books are sold

Acknowledgments

I published both ***The Druid*** and ***Death Series***, in 2011 with the encouragement of my husband, and continued because of you, my Reader. Your faithfulness through comments, suggestions, spreading the word and ultimately purchasing my work with your hard-earned money gave me the incentive, means and inspiration to continue.

There are no words that are sufficiently adequate to express my thankfulness for your support.

I truly feel connected to my readers. It is obvious to me, but I'll say the words anyway for clarity: a written work is just words on pages if they are not read by my readers. As I write this I get a lump in my throat; your enjoyment of my work affects me that deeply.

You guys are the greatest, each and every one of ya~

Tamara
xoxo

Special Thanks:

You, my reader.
My husband, who is my biggest fan.
Cameren, without whom, there would be no books.

WORKS BY TAMARA ROSE BLODGETT:
The BLOOD Series 1-6
The DEATH Series 1-8
Final Enforcement ALPHA CLAIM 7
First Species ALPHA CLAIM 1 (coming 2017)
Shifter ALPHA CLAIM 1-6
The REFLECTION Series 1-3
The SAVAGE Series 1-7
Vampire ALPHA CLAIM 1-6

&

MARATA EROS
A Terrible Love (New York Times Best Seller)
A Brutal Tenderness
The Darkest Joy
Club Alpha
One of Many (co-authored with Emily Goodwin)
The DARA NICHOLS Series, 1-8
The DEMON Series
The DRUID Series 1-10
Final Enforcement ALPHA CLAIM 7
First Species ALPHA CLAIM 1 (coming 2017)
Road Kill MC Serial 1-5
Shifter ALPHA CLAIM 1-6
The SIREN Series
The TOKEN Serial 1-10
Vampire ALPHA CLAIM 1-6
The ZOE SCOTT Series 1-8

About the Author

Tamara Rose Blodgett: happily married mother of four sons. Dark fiction writer. Reader. Dreamer. Home restoration slave. Tie dye zealot. Coffee addict. Digs music.

She is also the *New York Times* Bestselling author of ***A Terrible Love,*** written under the pen name, Marata Eros, and over ninety other titles, to include the #1 international bestselling erotic Interracial/African-American **TOKEN** serial and her #1 bestselling Amazon Dark Fantasy novel, ***Death Whispers***. Tamara writes a variety of dark fiction in the genres of erotica, fantasy, horror, romance, sci-fi and suspense. She lives in the midwest with her family and three, disrespectful dogs.

Connect with Tamara

*If you enjoyed **The Reflective Dissent**, please consider posting your thoughts, and help another reader discover a new series. Thank you!*

Never** miss a new release! **Subscribe:
Marata Eros NEWS: *http://blogspot. us3.list-manage.com/subscribe/post? u=84b2a95b50215894f9cc760c9&id=8c0cadb909*
And/or
TRB News *http://blogspot.us3.list-manage.com/subscribe/ post?u=ba35eacaa6103f3fbb7845efe&id=d832893c44*

BLOG: http://tamararoseblodgett.blogspot.com/

FaceBook: http://tinyurl.com/TamaraRoseBlodgettFB

Twitter: https://twitter.com/TRoseBlodgett

*Subscribe to my **YouTube** Channel: https://www.youtube. com/channel/UCMfERQYGL1lt0wCeX5Yvzxg*
Exclusive Excerpts!
Comedic Quips
*Win **FREE** stuff!*

Printed in Great Britain
by Amazon